HUNKPAPA
SIOUX

a novel

Richard L. DuMont

To Kaye

Best Wishes

Richard L DuMont

GELAN

Livonia, Micigan

Cover design, interior book design,
and eBook design by Blue Harvest Creative
www.blueharvestcreative.com

Published by Gelan
an imprint of BHC Press

Library of Congress Control Number:
2016958670

ISBN-13: 978-1-946006-21-9
ISBN-10: 1-946006-21-1

Visit the author at:
www.bhcpress.com

Also available in eBook

To Lolly

TABLE OF CONTENTS

HUNKPAPA
SIOUX

Chapter One
TRAVELING NORTH

The train was already twenty minutes north of Chicago and John still hadn't found a seat. This was his first train ride and he wanted a window seat where he could watch the prairies whizzing by. The shouting and talking of the passengers, the clicking of the train wheels on the steel tracks, the rocking motion of the passenger cars all added to John's excitement. He grinned, feeling a little foolish about the churning going on inside him.

John entered the third car and walked up the narrow aisle. The large canvas bag he carried proved cumbersome as he tried to pass the other travelers on the crowded train.

"Excuse me, ma'am," he said, as he banged his bag into a stout woman. She smiled broadly at him, lifted her handbag over his head, and squeezed by. He could smell a strong odor of whiskey as he continued down the aisle. Next, he came to a group of five men wearing cowboy hats. They sat around a makeshift table playing cards, each man eyeing the dealer suspiciously as he flipped the cards in front of them. There was more folding money and gold coins than John had ever seen. He pushed against the seats and slipped around them. A small boy ran into him and bounced backwards. Without stopping, the lad continued on, hitting the arms of the passengers. He would laugh loudly as the irate travelers jumped up and shouted after him. John watched as the youngster disappeared into the first row of seats.

Near the back of the car, John finally spotted two empty places; he was pleased that he would have the extra room for the long train ride still ahead. He slid onto the brown leather seat closest to the window and set his bag next to him. Gray smoke was blowing through the window and John pushed it hard with both hands until it shut. He brushed the soot off his suit, a gift from his mother last year on his sixteenth birthday. John leaned back in his seat and watched the Illinois prairie passing outside the train. The rolling grassland calmed him, and he soon noticed that most of the activity in the compartment had slowed down. The passing scenery, along with the gentle rocking of the train, seemed to lull the travelers into a subdued mood. John relaxed, stretched out his legs, and returned to staring out the window.

The quiet atmosphere was suddenly broken as a giant man pushed through the front door of the car.

"Hey!" he shouted. "Any seats back there? I can't find a damn seat anywhere on this train, and I'm gettin' awful tired of standing. I'm supposed to be ridin' to Minnesota, not walkin' there. By God, that conductor told me I'd have a seat and I aim to get one."

John sat up and watched as the newest arrival lumbered down the narrow aisle toward him. The man stood near six feet four inches tall, and John guessed him to weigh two hundred and fifty pounds. He wore the fringed buckskin of a mountain man and a wide-brimmed black hat. His hands and face were tanned deep brown. He stopped next to John's empty seat.

"Well, boy," he said with a broad grin, "looks like you win the honor of ridin' with the best darn trapper in all of Montana Territory. Move that bag of yours, so's a man can rest his old body."

John grabbed the bag and forced it under his seat. He straightened up and was pushed against the window as the big man sat down.

"My name's William Brunner," the mountain man said, extending his hand to John, "but just call me Rusty. It used to be my hair was red as a June sunset, but it's got kinda white lately."

John shook the man's hand firmly. "My name's John," he said. He could see Rusty had been a handsome man in his younger days, but his face was weathered and deeply wrinkled now. His chin was covered with a snow-white beard, which matched his bushy eyebrows, but, still, his blue eyes sparkled brightly when he spoke.

Rusty suddenly pointed out the window. "Ain't that pretty out there, Johnny Boy? God didn't make too many things prettier than the green prairies in the spring.

"I love the way the hills roll up and down so gently you hardly know they're hills at all. Why, I can remember when these plains went on for miles and miles without some sodbuster's place to ruin it. Look out there, boy. There's a white man's house everywhere you look and everythin' is dug up for planting. Didn't use to be nothin' but green buffalo grass for as far as the eye could see."

"It must have been beautiful," John said, without looking away from the window.

"It was," Rusty continued. "But there's still some free places like that even today, and that's where I'm headin'."

John turned and looked at Rusty. "Where's that?"

"Montana Territory," Rusty answered. "First, I'm riding this here Iron Horse up to St. Paul, and then I'll git me a real horse and head due west for some trappin' and huntin'. Can't wait to sleep under the stars. I been back East in Chicago for almost a year and I got to get away from all those people. I been sick for a month or so. I think it's from people fever."

He poked John in the rib with his elbow and laughed loudly. John smiled at the mountain man's joke.

"You know something, Rusty," he said. "After this train arrives in St. Paul, I plan on riding west myself. I'm going out to the Sand Fork River in western Dakota. Do you know where it is?"

Rusty ran a finger down his nose, trying to recall the place. "Yeah, I know Sand Fork. I trapped up there one fall until the Sioux ran me off. Beautiful place, but there's some mighty tough company up there. You plan on findin' that place by yourself, huh? I guess you been there before?"

John hesitated for a moment. "I've been there, but it was a long time ago. I was only five when I left, and, truthfully, I'm not so sure I can find it by myself. My uncle's out there, though, and I really want to see him.

"I was wondering," he continued, "if maybe I could ride a ways with you toward Montana and then I'd head off by myself. You could point out the rest of the trail for me."

Rusty scratched his head as he pondered the boy's suggestion. For some reason, he felt a liking for this young stranger, and he was worried how this pup would fare alone in the Dakota Territory.

"Before I agree, boy, there's something I want to know," he said. "Why in the hell would a white boy like yourself want to go to Sand Fork? There ain't nothing but Sioux up there who are just waitin' for nice scalps like yours. I'd say you'd last about a week at the most."

"You might be right, Rusty. But you don't know the whole story. You see, I'm a half-breed. My father was a Hunkpapa Sioux named Waukesha. My uncle, Iron Hatchet, is still roaming free, and it's him I'm going to visit this summer."

"I'll be damned," Rusty exclaimed, recognizing John's Indian features for the first time. The boy had short, straight black hair, bronze skin, and high cheekbones.

"I must be getting old, Johnny Boy," he said. "Just looking at you I can see Sioux all over you. No wonder you want to git out to Sand Fork."

"Can I ride along with you, Rusty?" John asked.

"Sure, I'd reckon I could use a little company. I might even be able to teach you a trick or two on the way. I suspect you ain't done too much ridin' and an old-timer like me could probably help."

They shook hands on the deal.

"Is your pa dead?" Rusty asked after a moment.

John didn't hesitate. "Yes, Rusty, he was killed a long time ago up by Sand Fork. I've been raised as a white boy in Chicago, but my mother taught me the Dakota language, and told me many tales of my father's people. I want to share in their way of life, at least for one summer. Sometimes at night, down on the lakeshore, I could almost hear the prairies calling me in the wind. It's probably like your 'people fever.' I found myself more and more alone, even though I was surrounded by people. I decided to head out west for a while and try to find my Indian relatives, the people of my father."

They were both quiet as the train gently rocked on. The landscape turned black outside the windows, and only the distant lights of an occasional farmhouse flashed by to remind them they were moving. John thought about the families inside the houses, and felt a sadness over leaving his mother. He lingered over that sweet and sad thought for a moment, and then pushed it from his mind. He turned back to his new friend.

"I guess," he said, "I should have tried somehow to tell my uncle I'm coming, but I'm sure it will be all right. He'll remember me just as soon as I have an opportunity to talk to him."

Rusty shook his head in dismay. "What if your uncle lifts your scalp first and then asks your name, Johnny Boy? You look just like a white boy dressed up like that."

"Don't worry," John said, "I still have my father's medicine bag and he'll know it when he sees it."

The old trapper was familiar with the Sioux's beliefs about their individual magic or medicine power. He watched as John unbuttoned his white shirt and pulled out a leather pouch that was tied around his neck with rawhide. John then put a handkerchief on his lap. He reached into the pouch, pulled out a dried prairie dog paw, and placed in on the handkerchief.

"My father's magic came from the small animals of the plains and the woodlands. The prairie dog showed him that, by being ever alert, he and his people would be safe."

From inside the pouch, John pulled out two bright orange beaver teeth and placed them next to the prairie dog's paw. "Once, at a time early in my father's life, he was resting by a small pond when a beaver proved big magic for him. My father, Waukesha, had been traveling far on foot, and he stopped to drink from a pond. The sun was warm and his belly full, and he soon fell asleep.

"He was awakened suddenly as a beaver smacked the water with its tail to warn him of danger. He lay perfectly still and opened his eyes slightly. Sneaking up on him was a Crow brave, the natural enemy of my father's people. This Crow had his face painted blue and red, and had drawn his knife to slay Waukesha.

"My father moved his hand slowly and found his knife. He suddenly jumped up, yelling his war cry. The screaming caused the Crow to hesitate in surprise, and my father rushed him. With knives slashing, they tumbled to the ground, rolling over, trying to stab each other. The Crow managed to cut my father's back, but finally Waukesha plunged his knife into the Crow's chest.

"The Crow warrior released his grasp and tried to stand up. He started chanting his tribal death song and fell back on the ground, clutching his chest. In a minute, his spirit left him for the next world.

"My father counted coup on his fallen enemy and sang his victory song. Before he left the pond, he thanked the beaver and Wakantanka for his life. Several months later, he was forced to take a beaver as food for his family, and the beaver's chopping teeth became part of his medicine."

Rusty was intrigued by the boy's knowledge of Indian lore. It was hard to believe that the young man had been raised in Chicago.

"What else you got there?" Rusty asked.

"The only item left in the medicine bag is dirt from the Paha Sapa, the sacred Black Hills of the Dakota. My father's people believe the hills are the source of all Dakota life, and every Dakota brave goes there as a young man to seek spiritual guidance. Waukesha was nineteen summers when he made his journey to the Black Hills in search of a spiritual vision.

"After reaching the Paha Sapa, he fasted and constructed a sweat bath that he made by pouring water on hot rocks inside a small tipi. He sat inside the steaming tipi, wrapped in a buffalo robe, as the sweat purified his body. When he felt himself cleansed, Waukesha left the bath and climbed further up into the cool forest of the Black Hills. His body was weak and he soon fell to the forest floor. While he slept, the vision he sought finally came.

"In his dream, he was standing alone on foot when a beautiful pony approached him, but my father refused to mount it. The pony nudged him with his head, but Waukesha would not ride it. Soon a light tan pony came up to him, but my father refused to ride this one, too. The same dream repeated many times, but Waukesha would not select any of these horses.

"At last, a pure white pony appeared in the distance. It approached cautiously, surrounded by a heavy mist. Waukesha knew immediately he must have this one for his own; he ran after it, but could never get any closer.

"Finally, he gathered all his strength and ran at full speed, making a desperate leap for the creature. He landed on the pony and shouted with joy at possessing this beautiful white animal. As he rode the horse triumphantly back toward the village, he realized he had lost his medicine pouch. He turned to go back and hunt for it when the trance suddenly ended.

"When he awoke, my father was filled with a strange mixture of joy and fear. He knew the dream meant he would someday achieve great joy, but the loss of his sacred medicine bag meant it would be very dangerous for him.

"He filled the magic bag with the precious dirt of the Black Hills and stumbled back down to his camp where he took food for the first time in four days."

Rusty had sat quietly, listening to the boy's tale of his father. He was always intrigued by the visions of the Plains Indians. They put great faith in them. He closed his big hands around the handkerchief and nudged it toward the medicine bag.

"Here, Son, you better put this stuff away. The conductor's coming to punch our tickets, and he might not understand why you're carrying these dead animal parts around."

Rusty watched as John put each item back into the medicine pouch.

"I know that Dakota visions have a way of coming true in a lot of cases. You can tell me to mind my own business if you want, but did Waukesha's vision come true?"

"Yes," John answered. "You see, the ponies in the vision all represented women. My father was a handsome man, very brave, and could have had his choice of Dakota women. But he showed no interest in the young Indian girls, and was always looking for the white pony of his dream."

John stopped talking briefly, but his thoughts raced on, and Rusty didn't disturb him.

"My mother was the white pony in his dreams. She was the daughter of a Quaker missionary who was working with the Indians of Standing Rock Reservation. My father went to the reservation occasionally for blankets and other gifts from the Quakers. The first time Waukesha saw the beautiful blonde girl, he knew she was the one: the white pony. When he told Iron Hatchet of his feelings, his brother tried to stop him.

"'The *wasicun* will not let a red man marry one of their women. It will only bring sadness to our people and to you,' he warned Waukesha.

"Waukesha gave in to his brother's pleading and stayed away from the Quaker's cabin. But, one day, while Iron Hatchet was away hunting, the Quakers rode out to the Sioux village with some fresh supplies. Waukesha was with my mother all day, but he did not speak to her of his feelings. His heart pounded wildly whenever she came close and he thought he would surely die if he didn't have her. Finally, the visit ended and she left the village.

"That night, when Iron Hatchet returned, Waukesha had made up his mind. He was going to ask her to marry him. If she did, they would live away from the village so there would be no trouble for Iron Hatchet's people. The two brothers argued violently that night, but my father's mind was made up. The vision would be fulfilled."

"So your pa actually married the Quaker's daughter, huh?" Rusty interrupted.

"Yes, he did," John said. "My mother often told me how she had admired the young brave whenever he came to visit, but she never thought seriously about marrying him. She was white, he was red, and marriage was unthinkable.

"She loved to tell me about the day my father proposed. He stood out on the porch, wearing buckskin and a full eagle feather bonnet. Mighty handsome, my mother would say. Her hands were trembling as she walked out into the daylight to talk to him.

"'Claire,' he called out, 'I know your father is gone, and I wish to speak to you.'

"'What is it, Waukesha?' she asked.

"He did not hesitate but looked her straight in the eyes. 'My heart soars like the Eagle whenever I am close to you, Claire,' he said. 'I am a man of few words. I wish to take you for my wife. I will provide food for you, I will not beat you, and I will father many fine children for us. Do not answer now. I will return when the sun goes down tomorrow. Whatever your answer is, I will understand.'

"My father mounted his pony and rode off quickly. He was sure she would refuse him.

"Needless to say," John continued, "she did marry him, despite her father's strong objections.

"Once Waukesha had asked her, she couldn't get the thought of marrying him out of her mind. It was as if her love had been in hiding and his proposal brought it out into the sunlight. She was a headstrong woman and once she decided that she loved my father, that was that. They were married a week later at the Sioux village.

"The marriage was a happy one for both of my parents. I was born about a year later, and Waukesha pushed the vision's warning of danger from his mind. But the sacred vision had not lied.

"When I was six months old, there was an incident in the white man's town. Four young braves had gotten drunk and were acting like fools. They grabbed a young white girl, and three of them held her while the fourth one tried to kiss her. The girl screamed loudly, and a group of angry townsmen rescued her, badly beating the four braves. Still, the white men were not satisfied. They thought these bucks were getting their ideas about white women from Waukesha and his wife.

"The following morning my father was missing from the camp. He had been hunting the previous evening and had not returned. At first light, Iron Hatchet headed up a search party to find Waukesha. Iron Hatchet was filled with a deep feeling of foreboding as they mounted their ponies." John sat quietly for a moment, his dark eyes misting slightly.

Rusty waited silently for John to continue, knowing the boy would have a hard time telling the rest.

John started speaking again, slowly. "An hour later, the war party found my father's medicine bag lying in the brush alongside the road to town. They dismounted and began searching the weeds, where they found his body. He was naked and propped up against a tree with his hands tied behind his back. He had been shot many times and his face and body were badly bruised. Iron Hatchet knelt down and untied his brother. He gently picked up the body and carried it to his pony, sliding his dead brother over its back. He turned his horse and walked it slowly back to the village.

"Iron Hatchet wanted to avenge his brother's murder, but the Dakotas had few guns and little ammunition. It would only bring more death to his people to attack the town. Soon, Iron Hatchet's small band moved west, away from the place of my father's murder, and out to Sand Creek, which is where I think they still live today. I am sure Iron Hatchet still bears a great hatred for the white man who murdered his brother."

John brushed back his tears as he ended his story. Rusty watched. The vision had come true.

"Did they ever arrest anyone for his murder?" Rusty asked.

"No, killing a red man is not always murder," John said.

"Yeah, that's the darn truth. Is that when you moved back East to Chicago with your momma?"

"No, not right away. Mother wanted me raised as a Sioux, and we stayed in the lodge of Iron Hatchet for five more summers where I grew up with my cousin, Little Horse. It was a fine time for me but hard on my mother. There was often trouble whenever the local whites found out there was a white woman living with the Indians. They were always trying to rescue her; once they even tried to force her to leave with them. These incidents were always tense and very dangerous.

"My mother's fear for the safety of the tribe persuaded her it was best to leave, so, when I was five, we snuck off, and the Quakers helped us return to Chicago. My grandfather was still living then and he took us in and helped raise me until he died. He left Mother enough money for us to get by on."

"Whew, Johnny Boy, that's some story and some life you've led. I reckon it will be a real interestin' trip to Dakota for both of us. I'm kinda curious to see the look on your uncle's face when I turn you over to him."

He winked at the boy, and they settled back into their seats.

As the train sped on through the night, a silence fell over the darkened cars. Most of the other passengers had fallen asleep after the conductor had collected their tickets and left the car. Rusty and John felt the gentle swaying of the train working on them and soon fell asleep, too. It had been a good day.

The noise of hissing steam and squealing brakes forced its way into John's sleep world. He opened his eyes, the bright light of the new day almost blinding him. Rubbing the sleep away, he looked out the window as the train slowed to a stop. Outside, two members of the train crew climbed up a ladder on a wooden water barrel and began pumping water into the locomotive. They were shrouded in mist as the steam from the engine swirled around them. Both men were laughing, obviously enjoying some joke.

Rusty's head suddenly popped up from the corner of the seat where he had been sleeping. "What's goin' on?" he asked, yawning. "We in St. Paul yet?"

"No, nothing like that. The train just stopped to take on water."

"Do you think we could get off awhile and stretch our legs?" John asked Rusty. "I'm feeling awful cramped and some solid earth would feel mighty fine about now."

"That sounds like a right fine idea, boy," Rusty said with a big grin. "Ain't nothin' feels better than mornin' prairie grass when it's still wet with dew. C'mon."

The two walked through the compartment and down the platform steps. The land was mostly flat and green, and the air smelled sweet after many hours inside the cramped passenger car. The two travelers walked slowly up a small knoll, the morning sun shining softly in their eyes, while in front of them the prairies rolled on and on, disappearing in the haze.

"My God," John whispered, "this is beautiful country. No wonder the Dakotas love their prairies. I can feel the earth calling me to stay here forever."

"You know, the Dakotas used to live here in Minnesota," Rusty broke in. "They was mostly Santees, and they lived here for hundreds of years until the white man drove them out in 1867. I can remember when they was here, though. It don't seem all that long ago.

"Now, the only Indians left is mostly up north. The Menominees, Winnebagos, and Ojibways have managed to hold onto some of their lands, but it's mostly frozen timber land that the white man don't want yet."

"You seem to know a lot about these parts, Rusty. Did you use to live up here in Minnesota?"

"Yep, sure as hell did. I came up here from St. Louis when I was a pup about your age; I went up north to St. Cloud and trapped. God, that's great country up there. I used to trap all up the Mississippi as far north as the Winnibigoshish Lake. Got along fine with those Ojibways, too. They knew a lot about surviving in the dead of winter—like how to make snowshoes and how to use a snowdrift to keep warm. Those days are still mighty darn pleasant in my mind.

"That's when I married a squaw woman, an Ojibway princess, and just as pretty a gal as God ever made. We was so happy at first. I'd still be there if things hadn't turned so bad."

John hesitated, wanting to ask the obvious question, but Rusty relieved him of his dilemma.

"It was a cold winter in the early 1860's when the bad breaks hit me. First my infant son died from an awful cough, and then my wife got kicked in the head by a horse and died three days later.

"Lord, I felt lower than a snake's belly. Only time I ever drank heavy in my life. I was drunk all the time, but my wife's kin helped me through the bad times until I got my right head back and was able to take care of myself. Soon after that, I left old Minnesota because the memories of my wife and child were too strong for me to stay.

"Just talkin' about them tempts me to head back up that way and see some of my wife's relatives. They were a proud and noble people once, but I wonder how they've taken to reservation life. Hey, Johnny Boy, it wouldn't take us but about a week up and back to see how the Ojibways are doing. It would be a good start for you're learnin' about the Indian people. How'd you like to go see Ojibway country with me?"

John didn't pause for a moment.

"That suits me fine, Rusty. I'm not on any timetable to get out to the Dakota Territory. It will be good experience for me to see other tribes, too."

Their discussion was suddenly interrupted by the hiss of the locomotive as the train prepared to pull away. The two of them ran to their car and hopped on board, laughing at each other.

The train gathered speed and rolled on north toward St. Paul. Inside the train, the two new friends continued discussing their plans while the hours flew past. Before they knew it, the train was slowing down as it entered the busy city of St. Paul, Minnesota, early on a May afternoon in 1875.

Chapter Two
SIOUX RELATIVES

The pre-dawn air felt chilly, even though it was mid-May, the Moon of the New Grasses. The wind blew stiffly from Canada, and the morning was quite cold. Little Horse, a young Dakota brave, pulled a blanket over his bare shoulders as he lay in the wet buffalo grass. He wore only buckskin pants; wearing a shirt was bad medicine when he hunted. Still, he hoped the sun would soon break through the trees to the small ridge where he hid. He had been waiting an hour for game to arrive at Running Turtle Creek, and his body was chilled to the bone.

Suddenly, the birds in the cottonwoods stopped singing. Little Horse knew something had disturbed them. He stared hard into the gray darkness of the tree-lined stream until he detected movement. His heart pounded wildly in anticipation.

It was a pronghorn antelope! Sliding his bow in front of him, Little Horse held it tightly, keeping it close to his body as he crawled through the tall buffalo grass. Moving slowly forward, he stopped to rise up and look. The antelope was drinking cautiously, its head bobbing up and down to watch for enemies. The brown and white animal moved nervously, ready to bolt into the brush at the first sign of danger.

Afraid of spooking his prey, Little Horse stopped advancing and crouched down. He decided it was time to rely on the wisdom of the Dakota elders to kill the pronghorn. He would use a hunting trick that had been taught for many generations, a trick that used the animal's natural curiosity to capture it.

Pulling an arrow from his leather quiver, he slid it across the bowstring as he slowly stood up again. He swayed his head back and forth like a pendulum, making his braids swing in a slow rhythm. Little Horse held his breath as he watched the antelope, fearing it would dash into the woods. But, the befuddled pronghorn did not move as the swaying brave came into view. The strange rhythmic motion fascinated the pronghorn and soon its head began moving in time with the young Dakota. Losing his natural caution, the antelope slowly walked across the creek toward Little Horse.

Smiling, the young man brought up his bow and aimed at the white chest of the antelope. He stretched the bowstring tight as the animal drew close. Little Horse released the string. The arrow shot forward and slammed into the pronghorn. Looking stunned, it stumbled backward and fell into the creek, thrashing in the water until it lay still.

The young brave jumped in the air and shouted in elation. "*Hoka Hey*! I have slain the elusive pronghorn. My family will feast tonight!"

He ran down the hill to the dead antelope, where he pulled it by its head and horns away from the creek. With water dripping from his moccasins, he sat down on a rock and spoke to the pronghorn.

"I am sorry to have to slay you, little brother, but my people need to eat. The Great Spirit sent you here to drink today so that I would find you. It was his will that you should die today."

After removing the arrow, he removed his knife from its sheath and slit open the antelope's belly. Plunging his hand inside, he removed the heart, which he placed on the grass as an offering to Wakantanka, the Great Spirit. After he removed the intestines, Little Horse slung the still warm body over his bare shoulders. He hooked the bow over his back and began walking toward the Dakota camp of his father, Iron Hatchet. As he walked, he sang of his joy at being a Dakota.

Nearing home, Little Horse crossed a small stream, the cold water swishing around his moccasins. He walked up the bank into the small village, which consisted of about 20 tipis, set up in a circle. The women were busy cooking and sewing, while the children ran and played around them. Most of the braves sat by their lodges, making arrows and talking. The village dogs soon caught the pronghorn's smell and, barking and yelping, they followed Little Horse as he approached his father's tipi.

Iron Hatchet stood in front of his lodge, a buffalo robe around his shoulders. Joy flashed in his black eyes as he watched his son carrying the large pronghorn to him. A crowd of women and children began to gather around them as Little Horse arrived and dropped the antelope at his father's feet.

"*Ho-Hoa*," Iron Hatchet shouted. "What is this? Has this great hunter slain the swift and elusive antelope by himself, or did he have help? Please, tell your father and our people how you managed to bring down this fine animal."

Little Horse spoke loudly: "Today I hunted with the good wishes of the Great Spirit. He guided me to the watering place of this animal. Then, relying on the wisdom of hunting, taught to me by my father, I used the natural curiosity of the pronghorn to slay him."

Moving his hands around now to better tell the story, Little Horse continued. "I stood up in front of the antelope, moving my head side to side like this." Little Horse began swaying his head back and forth. "Then the pronghorn started moving his head like this." Placing a finger on both sides of his head, Little Horse imitated the movements of the antelope. The entire crowd was now laughing and swaying with the young brave.

"Taking my bow, I aimed, and the arrow flew straight and true, and the antelope died with a surprised look on his face.

"That, Father, is how I killed this fine animal."

"*Hoa*, Son, you have made me very proud today. We shall feast tonight and the sweetest meat shall be yours."

The old man placed his arm around the bronze shoulders of his son and they walked past the crowd of happy Dakotas out of the village toward the pony herd.

The women of the camp would cut up the antelope, each getting an equal part. The wife of Iron Hatchet, Calf Woman, would get first choice, with the others then taking turns.

The boy and man walked through waist high buffalo grass, enjoying the warmth of the morning sun. They did not speak as they both enjoyed this rare moment of solitude away from the noise and daily activity of the village.

Little Horse was filled with pride. *How great to be a Dakota*, he thought. *Surely the Dakota are the favorite people of the Great Spirit.*

These beautiful hills abound with game; our ponies are swifter than the enemy's, and the women more beautiful than all other peoples.

Iron Hatchet nudged him roughly. "What are you thinking, young man?"

"Oh, Father, my heart swells with joy at being a Dakota Warrior. This valley of the Sand Creek must be the most beautiful place in all the earth. Our pony herd is large, and tonight our bellies will be full. A young brave could not want for more than this life."

Iron Hatchet wore a somber look on his large and wrinkled face. He chose his words carefully. "The Dakota people were always meant to live like this. To hunt, to fight our enemies, and to tell glorious tales of valor, such is the lifestyle of real men.

"But there is a dark cloud hanging over the face of the sun, even today. The *wasicun*, the white man, continues to violate our treaty lands because he is crazy with lust for the yellow metal found in our sacred place, Paha Sapa. I do not feel our leaders will let this continue much longer. Red Cloud is not so anxious to fight as in the Powder River War days, but Crazy Horse would rather die in battle than surrender the precious Black Hills. All Sioux life comes from those mountains and our nation would wilt and die without them.

"The long knife soldiers look the other way as their brothers cross into our lands to dig their precious gold. Something bad will come from this, and I worry for our people. Soon we will be drawn into another war with the whites, and many fine young braves will die."

Iron Hatchet walked silently for a moment. Then he resumed speaking. "I do not believe the serious fighting will start this summer. So I want you to spend your days hunting and fishing, and we will fill your evening with tales of our heritage and ancestors. We will hunt the buffalo together and later fight the Crows. You shall win your glory against them and be a man by the Moon of the Falling Leaves. In the spring, you shall be a full Dakota warrior and ready to fight the whites."

Little Horse listened attentively to his father, his mind racing on as he thought over Iron Hatchet's words. The white man was pushing his people again and he was worried about their safety. Perhaps the whites would drive them all from their ancestral lands someday. Little Horse knew he would fight the white man to the death if it came to war. The Dakota people would not easily give away the lands of their fathers.

"I will make you proud of me, Father," Little Horse said. "I shall enjoy this summer and be ready to meet the white enemy with no fear."

The two were now in the middle of the fifty-strong pony herd. Iron Hatchet currently owned eight horses. He stroked one on the muzzle, a fine brown and white pinto.

"How are you today, Swift Moon?" Iron Hatchet asked the pony. "You are the fastest, bravest pony a man was ever lucky enough to own. You are too fast for such an old man as myself."

He turned to Little Horse. "Take him, my son, for you deserve the best pony in our herd. Take him and he will let no harm come to you."

Little Horse stepped to the side of the animal and climbed on its back. His heart pounded in excitement as he held the reins and clenched his legs around Swift Moon's belly. This horse had long been his favorite and to own him caused his spirit to soar as high as the hawk.

"Truly, this gift has made this day the happiest of my life. I must now ride this pony and fly as fast as the West Wind."

Little Horse kicked Swift Moon with his moccasins. The horse responded and they galloped in a circle around the pony herd. Iron Hatchet watched as the two became one.

The boy and horse moved together in rhythm, the pounding of the pony's hooves beating the time. They circled the tribe's herd, the ponies becoming a blur of browns, whites, and grays. The wind sang around the face of Little Horse, his braids blowing out behind him. The air was cool and sweet as the lush green of the plains and hills whizzed by him. As the two thundered on, he was screaming. He was lifted from this world into a world known only to a young and free brave.

"*Hoka Hey*, Father!" he shouted. "He is a fine pony. I shall treasure him forever."

Chapter Three
THE MEETING

The fading sun cast long dark shadows over the two riders as they plodded along. Only the clopping noise of their horses' hooves broke the silence of dusk. The old man leading the way turned toward his youthful companion and spoke.

"Hey, Johnny Boy, what say we camp over there in those cottonwoods? There's a sweet water stream, and we can rest our saddle sores early tonight. It's been a long time since we left that gosh darn Ojibway Reservation and we need a rest. My old body is tired."

"Fine with me, Rusty," the boy answered. "I've been ready to stop for an hour."

They guided their horses into the cottonwood thicket and dismounted. John knelt down next to the creek and put his face into the cool, clear water. The cold chill snapped him awake, and he drank deeply, quenching his thirst. The water ran down his neck and into his shirt as he sat back on the bank.

The young man lay back and gazed up at the evening stars as they first appeared. The evening air was cool on his wet face, and a certain peace of mind settled on him. It was the first pleasant moment he had known for a while. The trip to the Ojibway Reservation had proven to be a complete disappointment for John and Rusty. The sight of the Ojibway warriors reduced to begging for government rations had sickened both of them.

When they had arrived at the reservation, they started looking for Rusty's kin. Because it had been ten years since Rusty left that part of the country, no one seemed to remember him. Still, they had searched through many filthy log huts until they came to the outskirts of the Ojibway village.

There a lonely looking old tipi was pitched back from the village under some large jack pines. Next to the tipi, an ancient red man sat alone, stirring an iron kettle with a large wooden spoon, his mind as far away as the smoke from his pot swirling into the air.

Rusty and John approached and Rusty called out to him.

"Grandfather, we are friends. We come looking for the family of Spotted Fawn, who was killed by a horse ten winters ago up near Winnibegohish Lake. Her father was Pigad, but I don't know what became of him."

The old man turned toward them, and they could see he was blind. He signaled with his hand for them to sit next to him. The two travelers sat down as the old Ojibway began to speak.

"Who are you white strangers that enter my camp? Perhaps you have come to harm the family of Pigad. Tell me of yourself so I know if you are truly friends."

"My name is Rusty, and my young friend is John. We have come to find Pigad or his family to try and help them. Spotted Fawn was my wife, and after she was killed I drank myself foolish that whole winter. Pigad's kin took care of me all that time and I never did get to thank them properly."

The old man reached out for Rusty's face and ran his wrinkled hand down his forehead to his chin. "Yes, I remember you, William Brunner. You have hair the color of the summer sun as it sinks in the

Western sky. You were a good white man, not like the ones we deal with now."

"I am William Brunner, Grandfather, but my hair is now the color of the prairies durin' the moon of the snows. I too have aged as you have, and I cannot remember your name. Do I know you?"

"Yes, Brunner, I am Pigad's brother, Red Hawk. I was older than Pigad but not as old as I am since the white man made us into beggars. We are like the camp dogs, grabbing for whatever scraps the white eyes throw us. I am glad I will soon join Pigad in the next world.

"I have known the joy of being an Ojibway warrior and can live on that until I die. My heart bleeds for the young men of the tribe who will only know the white man's ways." Red Hawk slumped as the despair of his thoughts weighed heavy on him.

"How did all this happen?" Rusty asked.

The old man slowly stirred his stew, filling the air with a pleasant aroma that wasn't familiar to John. Red Hawk mumbled softly and spoke.

"After the winter of the White Eagle Sioux uprising, the Sioux were driven from our land across the Father of Waters. We were pleased at first, but soon we learned that the white man was not to be satisfied with punishing only those Indians that had fought him.

"They came to us and many big powwows were held. Some of the chiefs licked the white man's boots and were willing to sell our lands for nothing. If we would stop hunting the buffalo and trapping lands for the beaver, we would be fed and taught how to farm. The peace parley went on for many days as the Ojibway were always hunters and we did not want to do it. Pigad was strongly against signing any treaty. But, after five days, several of the leading chiefs signed the paper. The white man kept reminding them of the fate of the Sioux and, above all, the Ojibway did not want to lose the land. Our father's bones are here and we want to join them when it is time.

"Pigad left the conference in anger because we gave away almost all our land. What was left was hunted out in the early years, and soon we found that our only source of food was the white agent. Our health is bad from the wooden cabins our people must live in. Despair is the mood of the young. Leave this place, William Brunner, for there is no one here that you can help."

Red Hawk stirred the pot, causing the liquid to splash and hiss as it ran down the side of the kettle.

"Our people fight each other for the meager rations we are issued. Pigad was killed four summers ago in a dispute over rations. I believe the agent had his Indian police do the cowardly deed, but it happened at night, so I cannot be certain. His food supplies were stolen, and the agent placed the blame on other Ojibways, and no one was ever brought to trial. That is white man's justice for the Ojibway."

John and Rusty listened intently to Red Hawk's story. They knew the Indians were being mistreated from their brief time in camp.

Red Hawk continued speaking. "Once all this land of clear blue lakes belonged to my people. Now, nothing is left but this small corner. It is sad to see my people withering on the vine, but the red man's days will soon be over and only the white eye will remain." The old man sighed deeply.

Rusty placed his hand on the old man's shoulder. He was gentle with Red Hawk, but he felt great anger and frustration about their plight.

"Grandfather, we are sorry to hear the sad story of your people. We would like to lend a hand, but ain't a darn thing that we could do that would really help. We will be glad to leave coffee and tobacco with you, but then John and I must go. My young friend is part Hunkpapa Sioux and we are ridin' west to the Dakotas to find his uncle and his band."

The old man's face lit up and he waved his hands excitedly. "Tell me, William Brunner, do the Sioux still live free on the plains of the Dakotas? I have heard of Crazy Horse and Gall who still fight the white man and hunt buffaloes, just like the old days. Oh, that is the life for a real man. If it is true."

"Yes, Grandfather, the Sioux still live as warriors, roamin' all of the Dakotas and even up into Canada. This young man seeks to spend a summer with them to learn the ways of his father. I believe it will surely make a man of him."

"Come to me, John, so I may speak to you," the old warrior said, motioning with his hands, and John walked next to him. Red Hawk pulled a pouch from inside his shirt.

"Take this. It is my medicine, and I will feel good knowing it will be on a free brave. Perhaps it will help you take a white scalp. It is no good to me anymore. Take it, and may the Great Spirit protect you."

John stuffed the leather pouch under his shirt. "Thank you, Grandfather."

"Will you share my kettle with me? I have not had such fine company in many days."

Although both were anxious to leave, they felt they had to honor the old brave by staying to eat. The meal was delicious, especially the meat, and John was surprised to learn he was eating dog. The thought of eating dog was somewhat unsettling, but there seemed to be no other option and so he continued eating it. During the meal, Rusty and Red Hawk talked freely of the old days, and all too soon it was time to leave. Rusty laughed heartily at the old man's parting words. The two headed west without riding through the Ojibway village again. Later, Rusty told him the old man's parting joke was that their meal had consisted of the pet bulldog of the Indian agent.

Rusty nudged John, and he suddenly awoke from his daydream by the bank of the stream.

"Hey, Johnny Boy! You gonna just lay there or help me make camp? I need to get some good shuteye tonight. If we ride hard tomorrow, we should be in Dakota country, and then we'll see some real Indians, maybe too damn many. C'mon, let's get goin' so I can go to bed."

Contrary to Rusty's estimate, the two men had crossed into Dakota Territory earlier in the day. They were being watched from the hills by four Hunkpapa warriors. The Sioux braves, wearing only breechclouts and moccasins, lay in the tall grass above the campsite. Manter, a veteran warrior, led these braves, but he was not sure what to do next. The white men were violating the treaty laws, and he could easily swoop down at night and destroy them. Still, he could not figure their purpose, for they were not miners after the yellow metal that drives white men crazy. They had no equipment for that, no mule to carry their supplies, no picks hanging from their saddle packs.

If they were buffalo hunters, they had no pack animals to carry off the skins. Yet, he knew they were not newcomers to the prairies since the old man rode as if he had spent many summers in the saddle. Manter felt there was something unusual about the young man, too. He would confront the two white men at dawn to hear their story before he killed them.

In the camp, John was deep in sleep when he suddenly heard Rusty shouting.

"John! Johnny Boy! You better git up, 'cause we got us some guests for breakfast."

Rusty's frantic shouting snapped John awake. Opening his eyes, John saw a tall Sioux brave standing directly over him and pushing a knife against his chest. John could see three other braves, including the leader, an older warrior who stood in the center next to the fire, holding a rifle on Rusty.

This brave spoke. "I am called Manter. This land you sleep on belongs to the Dakota people, and the Great White Father promised us that the whites will cross it no more. Now you must die.

"Still, it is a fortunate day for you because we are Hunkpapa, the fairest of all the Dakota. We shall listen to your story before we kill you. Let the old one speak first."

Manter sat down on his haunches and gestured for Rusty to join him by the smoky fire. Young John also sat down, next to Rusty. The Dakotas quickly tied their hands behind them with rawhide. Rusty started to speak to Manter in the Dakota tongue, though the old warrior did not seem surprised at this. His black eyes were fixed on Rusty's face.

Rusty spoke slowly. "Long ago the Sioux would not have tied me up before I spoke. I was their friend and trapped many winters in the Dakota and Montana Territories; but now I am treated like an enemy before my story is even heard."

"True, White Hair. For all whites are now our enemies."

"What of this young brave with me? He is one of your own people."

"Ha! He is a white man. Look at his clothes. Only a Sioux that licks the boots of the Indian agents on a reservation dresses like a white man."

"May I speak?" John asked in the Dakota language. Manter grunted in surprise as he heard his native tongue come from the young white man.

"Speak, young man, I am curious. But if you are Dakota, tell the story like a Dakota, not like a white man."

John smiled at Manter. "First," he said, "I must tell you of the joy I feel just knowing that I am among my father's people. The wind in the trees, the morning dew, all are bringing great happiness to me. Though I look white, I now feel like the Sioux that I am. My father was Waukesha, brother of Iron Hatchet. I have been raised by my white mother in Chicago, and I have come back to find my people and my uncle. If you kill us, you will be killing a brother Dakota."

John was almost breathless at the finish of his announcement. Perhaps these four braves would lead him to his uncle. The Dakota braves walked down the bank of the creek, where their ponies were feeding on the grass, to converse. Manter talked excitedly to the youngest brave. The discussion continued as they stood by the creek, pointing frequently back at Rusty and John.

"What's taking so long, Rusty?"

"Oh, no need to fret just yet. They still haven't decided what in the hell to do with us. Three of 'em would like to scalp us and be done with it, but the young one keeps arguing again' it. They ain't acting very Indian-like right now."

The four bucks walked up the slight grade of the bank to the campsite. The sun was now well up in the sky and it was going to be a warm day. A slight breeze rustled through the cottonwood leaves.

The youngest Sioux squatted down in front of John. He was about 16 years old, with shiny black hair tied in braids. "Tell me, what is your name?"

"John Holcumb is my white name."

"And do you have a Dakota name?"

"Yes, I was called Swift Pony as a boy."

The young brave's eyes lit up. "How long have you been away from the Dakota, John Hol-cumb?"

"About eleven or twelve years. I was taken to Chicago after my father was killed. Yours is the first Sioux face I have seen since that time."

These answers disturbed the young Sioux. "Do you know me?"

"I can't say I do," John said.

"I am Little Horse, son of Iron Hatchet and if you are Waukesha's son, we are cousins."

The words had been hard for Little Horse to say, for his hatred for the whites had grown that spring and summer.

John stood speechless. This Sioux warrior was actually his cousin.

"Little Horse, I remember now. We were born only months apart. We used to hunt buffalo calves and stalk rabbits together. Don't you recognize me?"

"I want to," Little Horse answered, "but I need more proof. Many winters have passed."

"Reach inside my shirt and you will find your proof."

The young brave grasped the medicine bag and lifted it over John's head as Manter came closer to look.

"*Hoa*," Little Horse exclaimed. "It looks like the medicine of a great Dakota warrior! Is it my Uncle Waukesha's, Manter?" He dumped the contents into his hand and showed them to Manter.

"Yes, Little Horse, the beaver teeth were strong medicine for Waukesha. He would go nowhere without them or the sacred soil from Paha Sapa."

Little Horse pulled his knife out and cut the rawhide from around John's hands, and helped him to his feet. "Swift Pony has returned to us from the dead. We must ride to my father's camp for a celebration!"

A savage yell rang from Little Horse's mouth. Then John shrieked as well, feeling great joy at being reunited with the Dakotas. "I am back home," he shouted, and tore off his shirt. It looked to Rusty like the four Sioux were now five.

"Come, Swift Pony, let's race," Little Horse yelled, and the two young men crashed into the trees and were soon out of sight. Only their wild yells and yelps could be heard as they ran for the sheer joy of running.

Rusty sat and watched quietly, knowing the Indians would soon remember him. He hoped his friendship with John would save him.

Manter walked over to Rusty and sat down, his dark eyes meeting Rusty's. "How have you come to be with this young brave, White Hair? Surely you are not from the East."

"No, Manter, I am not an Easterner. I met young John on the train and we sort of teamed up. I'm goin' to Montana country to hunt. Thought I might spend my last years up there. White men are not so common in those mountains."

"That is so, but it is the land of the Crows. Perhaps you will kill some of them for us."

"I don't kill nobody lessin' I have to. I believe God made us all, and I only kill his creatures to survive."

Manter mused over these words. "It is strange to hear these words from a white man's mouth. It is more like the talk of an old Dakota chief. Perhaps we will not kill you now but wait to let Iron Hatchet decide your fate." Manter took his knife and cut the rawhide binding Rusty's hands.

The two boys crashing through the trees interrupted their quiet conversation. John's face was now painted yellow and black as he ran to Rusty, his chest heaving, a grin spread across his face.

"*Hoa!* Rusty, I am home. Come on, let's ride to my father's village, and a feast will take place. My uncle will treat you as a guest of honor, and then you can go off to Montana. I will be forever grateful to you helping me find my Dakota family."

Chapter Four
THE CROW PONY RAID

Iron Hatchet's band was camped along a stream, known to the Sioux as the Little Turnip Creek. Its gently sloped banks abounded with wild turnips, a favorite food of the Plains Indians. Spring was a good time to be a Dakota for the grass grew high, game was plentiful, and the ponies were growing fat after a long winter in the Sand Creek valley.

The chief sat in front of his tipi, musing over the events of the last three days. His brother's son had returned to him from the dead, and surely this was a sign that the Great Spirit was smiling on his people. Iron Hatchet had assumed he would never see the boy again. The tribe was sure the Crow had taken Waukesha's wife and son captive in a night raid but no trace of them had ever been found. He believed the Crow had killed the boy and his white mother.

Iron Hatchet looked up into the sky and spoke. "Do not worry, Waukesha, for this time I will look after your son. He will learn the ways of the Dakota people and his medicine will be strong. I will teach him and make him a true Hunkpapa warrior."

"Calf Woman," he called out to his first wife, who was sitting with Chipeto, his second wife. "I am going to speak with the white man, Rusty. Find John Waukesha and Little Horse and send them to the old man's *wickiup*."

As he walked through the village, Iron Hatchet dodged several squealing little children. They were naked and laughed as they rolled a hoop past him. He was soon joined by his four dogs. They snapped playfully at his deerskin pants as he approached the small *wickiup* where Rusty was sleeping at night. The branches were packed tightly so the small house would stay dry through the hardest Dakota rainstorms.

Rusty sat nearby under a large cottonwood tree, smoking his pipe, a tin cup of hot coffee in his hand. The black pot sat on a stone next to the fire. Rusty rose to his feet as he saw the chief approaching. Reaching into his mess gear, he produced another tin cup and poured the steaming coffee into it.

"Here, Iron Hatchet, let this brew take the chill from the morning air."

Iron Hatchet drank deeply from the scalding hot cup. He groaned in pleasure, taking another sip before he spoke. "Of all the whites' inventions, surely coffee is the best. I will miss it when you depart from us for Crow country.

"I will also miss you, Rusty White Hair, for you are a true friend of the Dakota people. My heart is full of thanks for returning my brother's son to us. We will always be grateful."

"My pleasure. He's a good boy and I know you'll take good care of him. I got a present here for ya, Chief, before I go." Rusty bent down into his *wickiup* and pulled out a two-pound sack of coffee. He handed it to Iron Hatchet.

"Take this, I want you to have it. Tell your wife to use the grounds two and three times and it will stretch a good ways."

Taking the bag in one hand, Iron Hatchet grasped Rusty with the other. "Thank you, White Hair. It is too bad that all white men are not like you. May you have a good journey."

Rusty watched him walk away, the coffee bag swinging in his hand. Iron Hatchet and his dogs disappeared behind a tipi while Rusty started packing his supplies.

He washed his knife and fork in the remaining hot coffee and waved them in the air to dry. He rolled up his bedding and tied it behind the saddle. The precious coffeepot was washed in the stream and placed inside a small piece of canvas along with a big iron skillet and a bottle of castor oil.

He rolled the package up, folding the canvas tightly so it would not spill on the long trip. Placing the canvas supply bag behind his horse's saddle, he tied it down with rope, tugging at it with both hands to make sure it was secure.

"Now," he said, looking around, "where is that little son of a snake, John? He promised to come by and see me before I left. He's probably off pony racing again with Little Horse."

Rusty smiled in appreciation of the new freedom his young friend had found.

"Goddamn, it was good to be young," he said. "Well, I'll stop back and see him when I'm done up in Montana."

He climbed slowly into his saddle and moved the bay horse gently off toward Spotted Calf Canyon.

As the horse rounded a thicket of trees, he realized that he was being watched. He squinted into the bright sun and could make out two Sioux braves on horseback on the hill to his right, leading another pony. Rusty continued looking, finally recognizing Little Horse and John. The two boys gave out a whoop and galloped their ponies toward Rusty, waving in the air and yelling as they bounced down the hill. Laughing, they slid off the side of their horses as they reached him.

"Did you think you could leave without saying goodbye to me, Rusty? A Dakota is not a savage who forgets a real friend. I will miss you."

John reached up and clasped the old man's hand firmly.

"It's hard to believe that less than a month has passed since I sat down on a train next to a young white boy. Now, even your mother wouldn't recognize you," Rusty said.

John was wearing only a breechcloth. His hair was parted in the middle and hung down to his ears, still too short to be braided. His body was tanning from the hot prairie sun and he would soon be as brown as Little Horse.

Little Horse led a fine looking pony up to Rusty. "Here, White Hair, take this pony as a gift from my father and me. You have brought back my dead cousin to me and we will always consider you a friend. This brown and black pony is not so large as your horse, but he is a fine animal and will serve you well."

Little Horse handed the pony's rope to Rusty, who tied it to his saddle.

"Thank you, Little Horse, and thank your father for me. John, take care of yourself. I'll be back this way some day."

Rusty pulled his reins and his horse moved again onto the trail. "So long," he shouted.

"Take care of yourself," John called after him.

Both boys climbed on their ponies and sat, watching Rusty disappear behind the rolling hills. They turned their horses toward the Little Turnip Creek and trotted back to the village.

The first months in the Sioux village were a dream come true for a boy of John's age. All the adventure and outdoor living he had missed as a youth were now his. He hunted with Little Horse everyday as he learned to use the bow and arrow. His arrows flew wildly and missed everything at first, but his Sioux blood gave him the perseverance to withstand the other boy's chiding and he soon became adequate with this weapon.

His uncle gave him a gift of a pony, a tan horse called Panka. She was not as fast as Swift Moon, the pony of Little Horse, but her heart was good and John loved her. They flew over the hills together, at times in pursuit of game, at times in pursuit of the wind.

The annual spring buffalo hunt had already taken place by the time he arrived, but his uncle promised him that he would go on the late summer hunt. Anticipation of that adventure filled his days as he practiced his skills with the bow and lance.

One morning he was suddenly awaken by cries of two young boys.

"Crows! The Crows were here," they shouted as they ran past his lodge. John sprang out of his bed and crawled from his uncle's tipi into the dawn mist. Little Horse ran up to him, waving his arms.

"The Crows raided us last night and have stolen many of our ponies. Manter has lost his best war pony, and a raid on the Crow camp will take place for sure. Come, the council is meeting near Manter's lodge to decide what to do."

Little Horse filled in the details as they ran across the village. About ten Crow warriors had snuck into the sleeping Dakota camp and stolen over twenty ponies, even cutting the rope of Manter's pony from the side of his lodge. Such a deed demanded a counter raid.

When the boys arrived, the council and most of the village had already gathered. About 20 braves walked around, brandishing weapons and shouting for revenge. John had never seen the men of the tribe so excited, so filled with indignation that the Crow would actually raid their camp this far inside the Dakotas.

As the shouting gradually subsided, Iron Hatchet raised his hand and spoke.

"Manter, you and White Fox will lead the raid on the Crow camp. Pick your warriors well and defend our honor by returning with many ponies and a Crow scalp or two. I ask only that you take my son Little Horse with you so he may earn his Eagle Feather and be a man."

Little Horse shouted. "I will count many coups, Father, and bring you a scalp myself."

Catching the excitement, John shouted loudly. "Manter, take me too. I want a chance to prove myself."

"Yes, John Waukesha," Manter answered him, "you may go. Your father was a great warrior and I honor him by taking you. Prepare yourself with Little Horse and we shall set out when the sun is straight overhead."

Little Horse grabbed John by the arm and the two boys raced back to their uncle's tipi.

The raiding party, called a wolf pack, gathered at the village edge when the sun was directly overhead. It consisted of seven warriors and the two boys, all of them yipping and howling as they sat proudly on their ponies. Although he felt as brave as the rest of the raiding party, John couldn't help feeling a little afraid sitting on Panka waiting for the wolf pack to start off in pursuit of Crow ponies.

Manter was leaning over from his pony whispering with Iron Hatchet. They both nodded their heads and Manter sat up and spoke.

"Come, wolf pack, let us strike fear into the Crow's hearts. We will steal his finest horses and lift his scalp. Glory will be ours!"

Kicking his horse firmly, Manter's gray horse leapt forward and galloped out of the village. The other eight braves started yelling and their horses thundered off, chasing the speeding Manter. The small gathering of women and children watched as the raiding party became a dust cloud on the horizon and disappeared. Finally, even their shouts did not carry back to the village and the remaining Indians walked slowly back toward their tipis.

The war party gradually settled into a less rapid pace, the hot sun moving slowly before them as they rode through the rolling plains country of the Dakotas. It would be days before they found the Crow village.

Manter rode slightly ahead of John, wearing only a breechcloth with a large knife stuck in a rawhide belt. On his head was a beaver hat with two eagle feathers blowing behind him. His face was painted yellow and red to add to the fierceness of his appearance. He carried a lance and shield on one arm and a coup stick in the opposite hand.

Manter always rode in the center of the party while the others scouted ahead for signs of the Crow. The braves would leave the group for several hours, returning to report to Manter or White Fox what they had seen.

John waited for his chance to scout but he was never ordered into action. Finally he drifted back by Little Horse. "Will we get to go scout for the Crows, Little Horse?" he whispered.

Little Horse shook his head. "They will try to keep all the glory for themselves, and we must obey their orders for now. But every brave should have his chance for stealing ponies and killing Crows, and I'll make sure that we get our chance. Manter himself first counted coup when he was twelve summers by disobeying his father and chasing a wounded Crow warrior. By killing him with a lance, Manter became a man."

Little Horse's answer filled John's mind with anxiety. He had not thought about killing anyone. What if he had to kill a Crow? Was he that much of an Indian? He pushed the thought from his mind. He would help steal ponies and win his tribal glory that way.

After being on the trail for several days, John saw one of the Sioux warriors riding swiftly toward them from a ridge. It was Yellow Knife who galloped up to Manter and stopped as the dust swirled around them.

"The Crow are camped near the Rosebud Creek. It is a large village with many fine ponies and we can raid it at sundown."

"You have done well, Yellow Knife," Manter said. "You will have first pick of the ponies we steal tonight." Then, Manter turned to the youth and said, "John Waukesha, tonight we will teach you the proper way to steal the enemy's horses."

They rode on and stopped near a small stream to wait for darkness. Using the mud from the bank of the stream, they smeared each other's face and body. John smiled as he spread the wet mud over his cousin's back. He reached down into the creek bank and, bringing his hand up slowly, pushed the oozing mud onto Little Horses' hair as his cousin jumped away, shaking his head.

"So, you want to play with the mud, Waukesha," Little Horse said, reaching into the creek.

John took off running as his cousin came splashing out of the creek, both hands full of mud. John ran down the creek bank, cut across the water and up the other side into a stand of willows. Darting from tree to tree, he knew his cousin was gaining on him. He made a break for the creek but Little Horse grabbed him and they tumbled into the water. John tasted mud as Little Horse secured his revenge.

They stood up laughing as the creek washed the mud from their bodies. Putting their arms around each other's shoulders, they walked through the stream to the bank where the other braves had stood watching and laughing.

"Have my two mud wasps had their fun?" Manter asked in mock seriousness. The boys nodded in embarrassment.

"Good," Manter said, "then cover your shiny skin and stay quiet. When the sun is gone, we will ride."

Feeling a little foolish, the two youths again covered themselves with mud. They sat down on the bank together and watched as the sun slowly disappeared behind the hill. Growing anxious, they were relieved when Manter finally gave his signal to mount up.

Riding for less than a half an hour, the wolf pack stopped by some large rocks at the base of the hill. The sky was black now as they dismounted, and John heard Manter whisper his name.

"Yes, Manter, I am here," John answered.

"You and Little Horse must stay with our ponies," Manter said. "Guard them well for we will need them when we return. Your glory will be in the number of ponies we steal."

Gathering the ponies, the two boys led them into the rocks. John's heart felt heavy with disappointment as he watched the other Sioux braves disappear into the blackness of the hillside.

"Well," he said, "it seems we are to be left out of the real adventure on this raid. I guess there will be no Crow ponies for us this time."

"Perhaps, but maybe it is time we act like real Dakotas and raid the Crow pony herd ourselves. We can sneak around this hill, cut out a pony for each of us and still return before Manter. Then, when the sun appears tomorrow, we will have a good joke on the other warriors."

"But what if something happens to our ponies while we are gone?" John asked in a whisper.

"What can happen? We will only be gone a short while. Stop thinking like a white man. We must act now or never be warriors. Come, I am going. Do you stay here or become a Dakota?"

"I am coming."

The cover of the trees was soon behind them as they ran swiftly along the lower hill. John could barely see in the blackness, but he stayed close to Little Horse who moved along without stumbling. They started to climb now, moving up a small ravine, and the two braves soon reached the hilltop. The moonlight flooded the valley below where John could see the flickering lights of the large Crow village at the other end. The pony herd was directly below them.

"How many do you see, Little Horse?"

"Close to four hundred, I would guess. Come, we will move down there, through those trees where the moon does not shine so brightly."

The two disappeared into the pine trees, silently working their way down the hill toward the valley floor. John's stomach churned with excitement and fear as he followed closely behind his cousin. They walked through the trees for about ten minutes until Little Horse stopped in front of him. Dropping down on all fours, Little Horse signaled him to do the same. They crawled forward under the low pines, on the soft needles the trees had shed, until John could see they were at the edge of the pasture. The Crow pony herd was no further than twenty yards from them, grazing peacefully.

Little Horse sat back and leaned against a large white pine.

John joined him and whispered. "What do we do now, Cousin?"

"Do as I do from now on. Take out your rope and make a loop. Then we will crawl to the edge of the herd and pick out a pair of fine ponies for us. But we must be as quiet as the night owl so we do not scare the horses and bring the Crows down after us."

They inched out through the wet grass, moving four or five feet, then stopped to listen for the Crow. Only an occasional laugh from the village could be heard. Finally moving into the herd, Little Horse spoke softly to the ponies to calm them.

"Be quiet, Crow pony, and you will become a Sioux war horse." Slipping his noose over a brown horse, he whispered to John. "Take that gray and claim him as yours. I will lead mine back into the trees first and you follow when you no longer see me."

John slid his rope around the gray horse's neck and patted him. He watched nervously as Little Horse walked the Crow pony across the open field. Little Horse crouched down, leaning on the horse to conceal himself from the Crows. When his cousin disappeared into the darkness of the trees, John Waukesha started walking his new pony. The churning in his stomach had become a giant roar in his ears, as the moon seemed to grow as bright as the noon sun.

Surely, I will be seen and killed, he thought. Still, he continued on slowly, the trees growing closer and closer until he entered the dark safety of the pine forest. He walked the pony well into the trees, breathing a long sigh.

Suddenly a crashing noise came through the brush directly in front of him.

Little Horse is in trouble, he thought.

Tying the pony to a branch, he drew his knife and ran toward the fracas. The pine branches whipped his face as he ran but John knew he had to act quickly. Stopping short of the noise, he could see two shadowy figures struggling on a bed of pine needles. A Crow warrior was on top of Little Horse, trying to strangle the young Sioux. Little Horse twisted and turned trying to free himself, but the knees of the Crow pinned down his arms tightly. The Crow squeezed his hands harder as Little Horse gasped for air.

John watched the drama before him, almost in a trance, the anger flowing into him. He was a Hunkpapa Sioux and he would fight and even die to save his cousin. He would kill this Crow if necessary.

Sliding his hand up his knife handle, he swiftly crept up behind the Crow, his heart pounding loud and fast. Raising the knife high above him, he brought it down fiercely, cracking the back of the Crow's head with the iron handle. The force of the blow knocked the Indian off of Little Horse and John dove on top of the Crow. He cocked his fist to strike his enemy but the Crow did not move. John's first blow had knocked him out. John lifted the young Crow's head, his knife poised to scalp the fallen enemy. He held the knife there for a moment and then lowered it. John felt like a Dakota but not enough to scalp this boy. Perhaps he could have killed him in the fight, but not now. John bound the Crow's hands behind his back with rawhide and tied him to a tree.

Then, John ran back through the trees to find his Crow pony and steered him back to Little Horse. He slid his cousin on the pony's back, hands to heels, and led them away from the Crow.

A horse whinnied and John froze in his tracks. He tied the gray to a branch and moved in a circle toward the sound, where he found the horse stolen by Little Horse wandering in the trees. Leading both horses carefully, he headed back up the hillside toward the Dakota ponies. They moved swiftly, for John feared that Manter and the braves might have left them behind.

To his amazement, the Sioux raiding party had not returned and the horses still grazed quietly among the rocks. He led the two ponies in among them and slid Little Horse to the ground.

"Wake up, Cousin," John whispered. "We must be ready to move soon. Manter will be back any time now. Wake up."

Little Horse shook his head slowly. Finally, he spoke: "Am I in the Spirit World? Did they kill you too?"

"No, we are not dead, but we will be soon if you don't wake up before Manter returns."

The life returned in the Sioux's eyes. He could see the stolen ponies next to John.

"We did it! We stole two Crow ponies. But, how? How did we get here?"

"I will answer your questions as we ride back toward the village. Be still now. I heard something coming down the hillside and I must go see if it is our Dakota brothers. If they are Crow I will hoot like the owl and you lead the horses away from here while I delay them."

After entering the woods, John climbed a large pine and watched as the ghostly figures of the Sioux raiding party took shape. They were in possession of about twenty ponies, moving as silently as the mountain lion as they passed beneath him. They soon entered the clearing where Little Horse remained with the ponies. John could hear him exclaim.

"*Hoa!* White Fox, you have stolen plenty of the Crow's ponies. My father will be pleased. But where is Manter?"

White Fox spoke quietly, "Manter entered the Crow village to seek his stolen war pony, which was not in the large herd. We are to start riding east and he will join us.

"Where is young John Waukesha?"

John leapt from the tree and walked into the clearing. "I have been watching you," he said, "to make sure you were not Crows. I sat in a tree like an owl as you walked past me."

White Fox smiled broadly and spoke. "You are truly becoming a Dakota, John Waukesha, for we did not know that you watched us. But let us mount up and leave here before the enemy comes after us."

The boys scrambled onto their ponies and rode off behind their brothers. The band of Sioux warriors set a slow pace at first to reduce the noise. Only after several miles did the pace quicken so as to put distance between them and the Crow village. The rising sun would reveal their deeds to the slumbering Crow, and war parties would be sent after them in pursuit of their ponies. The more miles between them and their enemies, the greater were the chances of keeping all of the stolen horses.

The blackness of the prairie sky was giving way to light gray as the riders rode hard toward the sun. Spears of pink were flashing through the sky and dawn would find them with a good lead on their pursuers. John was feeling tired, but he was filled with an inner glow, for he had stolen an enemy pony and rescued his cousin. This had been a night he would long remember.

The sun was barely over the hills when Little Horse, who had been off scouting to the south, came riding hard toward them. He pulled his pony to a stop next to White Fox.

"Manter is approaching swiftly from below those ridges!"

"Do the Crows chase him?" White Fox asked.

"Not that I could see."

"Let us ride down to meet him then," White Fox called out. The Dakotas turned their horses southward, riding down the sloping ridge. Manter soon came into sight, moving rapidly across the plains, a trail of dust rising behind him. No Crow braves pursued him. He had gone south from the Crow village to lead them away from the rest of the Sioux raiding party and now was heading north to join his brothers.

John watched in fascination as the lone rider glided over the plains toward them. The wolf pack leader was leading one horse and riding his stolen war pony; his yelps could be heard as he neared the band. He was holding his war lance high, and John saw a black scalp tied to it.

Manter shouted, "I have the hair of the Crow who stole my pony! He fought bravely, but no Crow can defeat a Dakota! Come. Let us ride before his brothers catch up with us. We shall have many tales to tell when we get home."

The war party turned once more toward the rising sun, and rode off over the flat prairie. The trip back to the village of Iron Hatchet pushed both the men and ponies to the limits of their endurance. Several ponies dropped from exhaustion and were left behind. Manter did not want to be caught in the open prairies by a large Crow war party, so they did not stop to sleep at night, only resting for an hour or so, and then they were off again.

After four days of difficult riding, John was greatly relieved to see the friendly Dakota village in the valley below.

"It feels good to be home, doesn't it?" he asked his cousin.

"Yes, John Waukesha. I can see the women building a big fire for the celebration, and my father will be waiting for us with food."

Manter signaled to resume riding, and they rode down the hill into the village. The people gathered around the wolf pack, patting the stolen horses and praising the warriors for their thievery. The crowd parted, and Iron Hatchet walked directly in front of them.

"My people," he shouted, "let us sit and eat. While we feast, Manter and the others will tell us of their adventures on this Crow pony raid."

Iron Hatchet sat down on the ground by the fire, crossing his legs. The white haired elders of the tribe joined him as Manter strode proudly in front of them. He stopped before the fire and drove his lance into the ground. The Crow scalp hung from the high end.

"*Hoka Hey*, Dakota brothers!" he shouted in glee. "I have killed the Crow who dared to steal my war pony and I sent him to the Spirit World without his hair."

Manter grabbed his lance and ran up and down in front of the audience, waving the scalp as the Sioux clapped and shouted. He yelled war whoops as he ran a circle around the fire. He stopped again in front of the elders, catching his breath.

Iron Hatchet spoke loud enough for the whole tribe to hear. "Tell us Manter, how did you get this scalp? We grow anxious to hear of your deed."

Manter once again sank the lance into the earth. Crossing his arms, he walked back and forth in front of the elders as he spoke.

"White Fox and the rest of the wolf pack were sent down to the large Crow pony herd to steal their ponies. I knew a fine horse such as mine would be kept in camp, next to the lodge of the Crow who had stolen him. I had instructed White Fox to steal his ponies and then return fast to our village. He was not to wait for me for I would get my war pony back or die.

"I waited on top of the hill until the rest of the wolf pack moved down the valley toward the herd. Then, as swiftly as a timber wolf, I ran through the trees and into the village. The Crows slept deeply as I wandered around the village looking for my horse. The moon was bright, which aided my search, but made it dangerous for me. Finally, I saw my pony, tied to a tipi pole. I could hear the Crow inside sleeping and his hand was actually touching the rope outside the tipi.

"My heart pounded loudly as I slowly cut the rope. I watched the Crow's hand as I cut, ready to fight him. My pony was soon free and I grabbed the rope to lead him away.

"Suddenly, the hand disappeared. I thought I had awakened him, and I prepared to fight. But the Crow had not heard me; he only wanted to check on his pony. I leaned back against the buffalo hide on the dark side of his lodge. As the Crow passed me, I jumped on his back, covering his mouth with my hand, as I plunged the knife into his chest. He stiffened against me and fell limp into my arms. Only a hissing sound came from his mouth. He was dead. Dragging him into some weeds, I scalped him and counted coup. One less enemy for the Dakotas.

"I led my pony quietly from the Crow camp and rode due south. I knew the Crow would find the body at first light and, by heading south, it would give White Fox extra time to get a good head start. I rejoined the wolf pack later that day and, by riding fast, the Crows never caught us. There must be great wailing in the Crow village tonight, Iron Hatchet."

Manter once more raised the scalp and, walking slowly with his chest stuck out, he received the cheers of the tribe members.

Such is the glory of being a true Dakota warrior, thought John. The other members of the raiding party then took their turns in the telling of their adventures. John listened as White Fox spoke first and then the others. The shortest story came from Laughing Man, one of the braves John didn't know very well. His account was simply this: "We steal many fine ponies, while the Crow never leaves its nest."

When all the braves were finished, Little Horse jumped up and stood in front of Iron Hatchet.

"Father," he said, "may I speak? For although we were left to guard the horses, we too have proven ourselves to be Dakota braves."

"Yes, go on," Iron Hatched answered.

"First I have a surprise." The young buck ran quickly through the circle of Hunkpapa Dakotas behind a large tipi.

John watched his cousin return, leading the two Crow ponies they had stolen. He walked proudly, relishing the moment. As he re-entered the circle, he motioned to John.

"Come, John Waukesha, you will share my story."

John walked into the center and the two boys climbed up on the ponies' backs. After looking around at the expectant faces of his people, Little Horse continued speaking.

"These ponies were not taken from the Crow by the others, but by John Waukesha and me. We snuck into the far end of the herd and took them from under the very noses of the Crow.

"Come, White Fox, Yellow Knife, Three Fingers, and see if you can claim these ponies as stolen by yourself."

The members of the wolf pack walked to the youths and carefully inspected the horses. They patted and rubbed the ponies looking carefully at them. After some lively discussion, White Fox turned toward Iron Hatchet.

"The boy speaks the truth, Iron Hatchet. None of my braves know the markings of these animals. They were not taken by us."

Iron Hatchet's eyes glowed at this news. He waited until the wolf pack sat down on their mats with the others.

"What true Dakota braves you two have proven to be," he shouted for all to hear. "You have filled my heart with joy. Tell us of this brave deed so we may share in your triumph."

Iron Hatchet listened intently as his son related the story of how they had stolen the horses and fought off a Crow before escaping. He did not flinch as he told of John rescuing him, but Little Horse also said he could have finished off the Crow by himself.

John smiled. Now they could both have their glory.

Iron Hatchet moved forward and stood next to John. "You have come back from the dead, John Waukesha, to save my son from death. The Great Spirit smiled the day you returned to us. You are now a full Hunkpapa Dakota and have made me proud. From this day forth, you also are my son."

"Thank you, Iron Hatchet. A Dakota could not ask for a better father. I am filled with pride to be called your son."

Iron Hatched was obviously pleased with John's words. He grasped John's hand and then hugged him, patting him on the back.

"Tell me," Iron Hatchet said, "where is the scalp of the Crow you knocked off of Little Horse?"

"I wish I could give it to you," John answered, "but when I went to help Little Horse, the Crow had already snuck off into the forest like a snake. I thought I had better get Little Horse away before the other Crows were alarmed."

Iron Hatchet spoke: "Your glory lives in the life of Little Horse. He owes you his life, and this is the closest bond among men. You have helped steal two fine ponies and you may keep yours. But tomorrow, I will give you one of my finest ponies, for you are a Dakota warrior now and should have only the finest of horses."

"Thank you again, Iron Hatchet," John answered, "and I also wish to make a gift. This Crow pony I sit on shall belong to Manter. He brought me here to my people and he took me on the pony raid that made me a Dakota warrior."

John slid off the pony and led him to Manter, where he handed the warrior the reins, and stepped back. Manter patted the animal on the neck and ran his hand through the pony's mane.

"Thank you, Waukesha. Your father would have been proud of you this day. You have pushed aside your white ways in a short time, and are now a Dakota."

John walked back into the circle next to Little Horse, and climbed up behind his cousin on the Crow pony.

"Come, Little Horse, let's return to our lodge. It has been a long day and I am very tired. We will sleep well tonight."

Little Horse gently turned his pony and walked it slowly through the crowd. "Yes, Waukesha, it has been a long day, but such a great day to be a Dakota!"

Chapter Five
THE BUFFALO HUNT

John's summer with the Dakotas passed quickly; the days were filled with horse racing, hunting, and swimming in the Little Turnip Creek. He lived in the lodge of Iron Hatchet and spent many evenings listening to the men of the tribe telling tales of valor and glory when fighting the Crows and, more recently, the white men. The great buffalo hunts of the past were also vividly recounted, and these discussions made John eager to join the upcoming fall hunt.

In the Moon of Leaves Turning Yellow, the Hunkpapas were preparing to join several other Sioux bands in the hunt. John was sitting in his uncle's tipi making a spear when Iron Hatchet entered. The older Sioux walked next to him and sat down, crossing his legs, while John waited for him to speak.

"John Waukesha, you are like a true son to me," he said slowly. "This summer with you here has been a happy time for me. But when you came to us, you talked of staying for only one summer and now the Moon of Falling Leaves is upon us and you have not stated your plans. I wish that you would stay with us for many winters, never to return to the whites. Do you know your plans yet?"

John rotated back and forth on his haunches, choosing his words carefully.

"I have never been happier in all my life, Father. I wish to stay for the great buffalo hunt, as I need to hunt the buffalo to be a true Dakota. I have much to learn yet, so I will stay until at least next summer."

"That is fine, John Waukesha, but what of your mother?" Iron Hatchet asked.

"Can I get word to her? If it is possible, I would like to write her so she does not worry about me."

"Yes, write the white man words on paper and it will be taken to the *wasicun's* trading post to start its journey toward the rising sun. You will feel better after sending it." Iron Hatchet stood up and walked through the entranceway, disappearing through the flap.

Three days later, a Sioux rider visited the village at dawn and Iron Hatchet declared it time to move camp. By noon, the village was mobilized and started southwest across the prairies for the fall buffalo hunt.

Riding his pony ahead of the travelling village, John's thoughts were on the hunt. He had sent a letter two days earlier to his mother, announcing his intention to stay with the Dakotas for a full year. He knew his mother would approve and understand his decision, probably knowing all along that he might not be back as planned.

But even his mother might not have recognized him as he rode with the tribe toward the Black Hills. Waukesha's black hair was still not shoulder length, but he wore it in braids, with an eagle feather stuck in the back. His skin color was close to that of the other Hunkpapas, due to the hot prairie sun burning it a deep tan. Carrying a war lance in his hand, he looked very much like every other brave on the march. He was handsome, his dark eyes alive and sparkling whenever he laughed, and more than one Dakota maiden had cast an admiring glance at him when he rode by.

Seven days on the trail had past when Little Horse and John reached the top of a rise and pulled their ponies to a stop. Spread out in the valley below was the biggest Sioux encampment John had ever seen. It was ten times as large as Iron Hatchet's village. The entire valley was covered with tipis and *wickiups* arranged in clusters, most with ponies tied next to them. Smoke hung heavy over the entire village. The grass was already eaten away and dust swirls could be seen where the Dakota children played. John was surprised to see a number of stolen U.S. Army baggage wagons in the encampment being used as play areas for the naked Indian children. Of course, the usual number of dogs roamed the village looking for scraps.

The two young braves rode down the hill toward the village.

"What tribes will be here, Little Horse?"

"There will be mostly Oglala and Hunkpapa Sioux, but the Minnieconjou will also be here. I would not be surprised to see our friends the Cheyenne here, as they often join us for this hunt."

"You must make sure I meet them all. I want to know all my Indian brothers," John said.

"There will be one great leader here that you may get to meet, Waukesha. The great Oglala leader Crazy Horse will come on the day of the hunt, and maybe Iron Hatchet will be able to arrange a meeting for us."

"I would consider that a great honor," John answered. "I heard of Crazy Horse even when I lived in Chicago and now I may meet him. *Hoka Hey!*"

The next day, John, Little Horse, and a young Cheyenne named Snake headed out of Iron Hatchet's camp to scout for the buffalo herd. They would search for buffalo trace that had been worn deep over the years, as these were the usual routes taken by the herd. The trio raced their ponies south and east, the village soon disappearing behind them. Slowing down their pace, they spread out, the Cheyenne moving off toward the left and Little Horse to the right. Several hours passed as the boys moved across the plains, the sun warm on their faces. John enjoyed the gentle swaying movement of his pony and soon he was daydreaming.

A rumble from the distance slowly forced its way into John's consciousness as it grew louder and louder.

Thunder, John thought. *Can that be thunder?* He looked in bewilderment at Little Horse, who was riding quickly toward him, yelling and waving excitedly as he approached. As the roar grew louder, John could hardly hear what his cousin had shouted.

"Come, the buffalo are here. *Hoka Hey!* It is a fine day to hunt!" With John chasing after him, the Sioux brave kicked his pony and rode off toward Snake. He could feel the roar growing as they approached Snake, who was standing on the ground looking down the valley.

John Waukesha and Little Horse reached the peak of the hill together. The valley below thundered up at them as the black mass of a huge herd rumbled by, shaking the earth beneath their feet. The buffalo herd stretched beyond the horizon, so neither the end nor the start could be seen.

"Magnificent!" John exclaimed. "I would not have believed this without seeing it. The buffalo herd is so large. This herd could feed our village for many winters."

"Yes, Waukesha, there will be good hunting tomorrow," Little Horse answered. "Let us ride back to the village and tell of our discovery."

Dawn of the next day found the camp alive with activity as the warriors prepared their weapons for the hunt. Some had bows or lances but there were a few rifles, which were the prized possessions of their young owners. Many of the older Indians preferred their bows to the white man's rifle; Iron Hatchet was one of those, who favored a war bow made of ash and strung with two buffalo sinews twisted together. He proudly carried it over his shoulder in a buckskin case, which was decorated with fringe and beads of red and yellow. He was placing arrows in the quiver when John Waukesha asked him about it.

"Tell me, Father, why do you still use the bow and arrow? Is the white man's rifle not better?"

"For some it is, but for me there is nothing better for the hunt than my bow. It is accurate at a hundred yards and I can load it and shoot much faster than the musket or single shot rifle. It is as quiet as the hawk in flight and does not cause the buffalo to stampede when I shoot. It makes me sad to think that the young braves do not know how to use the bow, but I have to admit that the white man is much better at making weapons for killing than the red man. Even I carry his knife made of steel."

The old chief slung the arrows over his shoulder.

"Come, John Waukesha, Little Horse, let us join the others. We ride soon and this hunt must be successful so our winter will not be hard on us and our children."

The three left the lodge and mounted their ponies, John on Panka and Little Horse astride Swift Moon. They were their finest ponies and would have to carry them well that day, as a buffalo hunt could be very rough on an Indian pony. Joining the other Hunkpapa braves in the pre-dawn darkness, a hush fell over them when the Oglala warriors rode in.

"He is here," Little Horse whispered. "Crazy Horse is here. He rides at the head of his hunting party."

John turned as the Oglalas joined them and, to his amazement, Crazy Horse passed within four feet of him. He was surprised to see that the famous Oglala Chief was not a tall man, actually being shorter than John. Crazy Horse was wearing a red and black hawk head in his hair and his face was painted with red and black lightning streaks, for he could not be harmed when he wore this medicine. Crazy Horse rode by and all the Dakotas fell in behind him without a recognizable signal from their leader. John knew it was time to start the hunt and, riding to the front of the party, he was joined by Snake and Little Horse. As an honor for finding the herd, the three young men would lead the Dakota and Cheyenne hunting party as it rode out from the village.

Reaching the herd about mid-morning, the Sioux found the buffalo grazing in many small groups. The hunting party separated into two columns and rode down the hill toward a herd that consisted of about one hundred animals.

Because John had never seen a hunting surround before, he stayed close to Little Horse while the braves of the two columns encircled the herd. It was a trapping technique used for many years by the Plains Indians. The buffalo did not try to run but formed their own circle of defense with the calves in the middle. They stomped their hooves into the dirt and snorted warnings at the Indians.

John's heart was thumping as he turned Panka toward the buffalo. He assumed they would merely sit where they were and shoot the prey but he should have known better. That would require little or no courage and the buffalo was an opponent worthy of being met head on.

Suddenly, an Oglala warrior broke from the circle and rode his pony directly into the buffalo herd with a raised lance. Plunging the lance into the side of a large bull, the enraged animal rammed its head into the Sioux pony and tore open its side. The horse fell down, pitching the rider into the panicked herd. The brave struggled to his feet and miraculously managed to escape to his brothers. A series of these individual attacks then took place, each brave trying to outdo the others. The wounded buffalo were fighting furiously, goring anything that was close, including other buffalo. Some terrified calves darted from the circle and were finished off by the Sioux who waited on their ponies.

However, the buffalo were not the only wounded, for the arms and legs of several Sioux were torn open by the huge buffalo horns. The animals were fiercely protecting their young and would not yield easily. John watched in fascination as the kill continued; as another bull fell dead on the ground, the air was filled with yelling.

The animals bellowed in defiance, but were doomed because they could not escape.

Suddenly, a large bull broke from the herd and ran directly at John, causing him to freeze for an instant. The huge animal bore down on him, and he pulled Panka aside as the animal's horn caught his buckskin breeches and tore them. John turned his pony after the escaping buffalo and the hunt was on. He would kill this beautiful creature so his people could eat, and he could become a true Dakota hunter. Hooves pounding loudly, the swift pony gained on the thundering bull as John shouted with joy. His horse galloped on until the buffalo was next to him, turning right and left, trying to escape. John raised his lance high and as Panka drew next to the bull, he hurled it with all his might, sinking it deep into the buffalo's hump.

But the animal kept running, though more slowly, bleeding badly from the wound. Waukesha followed on Panka, when, suddenly, Little Horse galloped past him, riding right next to the buffalo. His cousin pushed his lance deep into the wounded bull's side and let go.

With this, the huge beast stopped running and stood shakily on all fours. His tongue hanging out of his frothing mouth, the bull bellowed loudly and sank down on his knees. Raising his bearded head once more, the buffalo bull rolled slowly on his side. He snorted one last breath, blowing dust out from his mouth and nose. His tongue drooped out and he was quiet.

John Waukesha slid off Panka and approached the dead buffalo with Little Horse. Thrilled to his very soul, he hugged his cousin. They both climbed up on the buffalo's side and Little Horse shouted: "*Hoka Hey*, brothers. We have killed a mighty buffalo. We are now true warriors! *Hoka Hey!*"

Little Horse and John sat down on the carcass. John ran his hands through the buffalo's curly black mane.

"You are such a magnificent animal, Brother Buffalo. We are sorrowed by your death, but it must be this way in order that our people may live," John said.

"We will leave your heart on this prairie as is the Dakota custom," Little Horse said. "It will insure us that next spring your brothers will come back to us."

Little Horse turned to John and said, "You shall have the hump to eat for your own, and the women will make you a blanket from its hide for this winter.

"But now, we must finish the hunt. Pull your lance from his back and rejoin the circle."

Little Horse pulled out his lance, climbed on Swift Moon, and raced back to the others. John patted the dead buffalo once more, struggled as he pulled out the spear, and returned to the surround. Nearly a hundred buffalo now lay dead on the grass as the Dakotas walked among the carcasses, finishing off any that were still alive. The braves chattered constantly, bragging on their exploits and daring and showing one another their wounds.

When the women began to arrive from the village to dress the buffalo, the older warriors rode off to the village while John, Little Horse, and about twenty other younger braves remained behind to guard the kill. They would also be needed to help the women load the wagons. Several hours passed and the buffalo bodies were packed on the war wagons or ponies for the trip to the village. Only the buffalo hearts were left on the prairies as an offering to the Great Spirit for the successful hunt.

Upon returning to the village, the Dakota women immediately started preparing the buffalo meat by cutting it into strips to dry for eating in the winter. After skinning John's buffalo, Calf Woman, the wife of Iron Hatchet, stretched out the skin on the ground. Using a rock, she drove in pegs to secure it. She knelt down, bent over the skin, and started scraping off the meat and fat with remarkable speed as the stone flesher cleansed away the buffalo meat. She sang softly as she worked, the autumn sun warming her back.

John sat down next to her, crossing his legs and spoke. "May I watch? I have never seen it done before."

"Yes, John Waukesha," Calf Woman giggled, "but watch out, for the meat flies everywhere when I work."

Calf Woman started humming again, her hands working quickly. She was joined by her younger sister, Chipeto, a fat woman about thirty-five summers who was Iron Hatchet's second wife. Customarily, the Dakotas had several wives; the more wives and people a man supported, the greater he was in the eyes of his tribe. The two women worked away and soon changed to another scraper of stone, which cleaned away more of the fat remnants. Then the two women ran their hands over the hide to insure it was clean.

"Look, John Waukesha," Calf Woman spoke to him, "it is now ready to be tanned. You may watch us start, but days will pass before it is finished. We need to soak it several times and scrape it again until it is tanned. Then I will decorate it so it will be a proper robe for a son of Iron Hatchet."

"Thank you," John answered. "I will be proud to wear it."

Calf Woman sent Chipeto to fetch the tanning liquid from Iron Hatchet's tipi. It was a fresh batch the portly woman returned with.

"What is it, Calf Woman?"

"It is the fluid that makes the hide soft," she answered. "It is made from the brains and fat of the buffalo."

John screwed his face up at that announcement and decided it was time to depart.

Many days passed before Calf Woman presented him with his buffalo robe, which was beautifully decorated with beads on the front and porcupine quills sewn on the sleeves. The inside was painted with red stripes. John slid it over his shoulders and knew it would keep him warm this winter.

"Thank you, Calf Woman," he said to her. "You've done me a great honor by making me this fine robe. I can now face my first Dakota winter with no fear of freezing."

The old woman smiled at his words, as they were all she needed. She turned around in the tipi and began humming a song as she prepared supper.

The warrior clans began leaving the huge encampment through the next week and headed toward their winter campgrounds. John and Little Horse hung around the Oglala camp the morning that Crazy Horse was to depart. They could see the famous chief sitting next to a fire, warming himself, as he talked with several sub-chiefs. Some of these chiefs would take their clans back to the reservations at Pine Ridge or Standing Rock for the winter, but Crazy Horse would spend his in the wild, near Bear Butte by the Black Hills.

"Can you hear what they are saying?" John asked Little Horse.

"Not all of it, but they are making plans to meet next spring up near the Rosebud and Greasy Grass Rivers. Crazy Horse feels there will be real trouble with the white man next year, and so they want all the Sioux and Cheyenne to be there. They will send word to Sitting Bull, Gall, and Two Moons of the Cheyenne to be there."

"Do you think they will all come?"

"I don't know, but my father says a fight with the whites is coming, and we Dakotas had better be united."

The conference they had been watching started to break up. The sub-chiefs waited until they were sure Crazy Horse was finished before they left. The Oglala camp was ready to move and Crazy Horse mounted his pony. The *travois* and wagons rose dust, which soon obstructed Crazy Horse from view, as John and Little Horse watched the legendary chief vanish beyond the horizon.

The Hunkpapas broke camp the following morning and headed northeast, as Iron Hatchet had decided to winter near Cedar Creek. The area was well forested to protect them from the north winds, and the Hunkapapa Reservation, Standing Rock, was close enough so that his people could go there to draw rations. After all, Iron Hatchet did like his coffee. The Indians would be issued blankets and other basic necessities. In addition, the Quakers would give them pants, coats, and hats.

Winter settled in soon after the Sioux arrived at Cedar Creek, and it was now the Moon when the Snow Drifts. Life in the village drew to a virtual standstill. Only an occasional brave ventured out to test the bite of the cold north wind, as the warm coziness of the tipi became the center of activity. This consisted mostly of telling tales of bygone days and eating *pemmican*, the dried meat of the buffalo. John, Iron Hatchet, Calf Woman, Chipeto, and Little Horse spent many hours in conversation. The women worked while they talked, usually decorating a robe with beads or stroking their long black hair with a porcupine comb. The two were very curious about John's life in Chicago. They were always trying to get him to tell them about it.

As Chipeto put buffalo chips on the fire, she would ask Calf Woman, "I wonder how the white people warm their wooden houses in the winter? Surely there are no buffalo left in Chicago. Do you know Calf Woman?"

"No, Little Sister," she answered, "I do not know. Maybe they burn the wood of the houses."

"No, no, they don't do that," John said. He was smiling at their veiled attempt to pry information from him.

"The white man's wooden cabin is heated by a large black iron stove that burns wood or the coal that comes from the earth. The fire burns inside the stove, giving warmth to the house and heat for cooking."

"What is coal?" Chipeto asked.

"It is a black rock taken from the earth far east of here and burns better than the buffalo chips," John said.

"Whoa, Waukesha," Iron Hatchet said, jumping into the conversation, "you mean the white man can burn rocks? That is hard to believe."

"It is true. It is with this coal that the fire is made hot enough to forge the steel made into the knife you carry. It is the coal that is used to feed the Iron Horse as it rumbles across the prairies."

"Now I know of what you speak," Iron Hatchet exclaimed. "I have seen this coal myself one time several summers ago when we stopped a train for our rations from the agent at Standing Rock. It is large black rocks and very soft."

"Yes, Father, that is it."

This seemed to satisfy the women's curiosity for a while. John smiled to himself, knowing they would question him again.

John had calculated the date since his arrival at Iron Hatchet's village. He reckoned it to be late January 1876, and he had missed Christmas and the holidays with his mother. He thought more often of her now that he was confined to the tipi. Feeling guilty, he wrote her a letter:

> *Dear Mother,*
>
> *Boy, I used to think it was cold in Chicago but this winter on the Dakota Plains is unbelievably cold. The snowdrifts are six to eight feet high and we have to go brush it off the tipis or it will cave in the sides. The buffalo hide won't tear but the lodge poles might crack from the weight.*
>
> *I participated in a buffalo hunt in the fall and actually killed a large bull. Not too bad for a Chicago boy. Iron Hatchet was very proud of me and I think father would have been, too.*
>
> *Iron Hatchet and Calf Woman watch out for me as if I were their own son, and Little Horse is like the brother I never had. I have learned much about my Sioux ancestry, but have much yet to learn.*
>
> *There will be a huge gathering of all the Dakota tribes up in Montana in the spring and I am going. Crazy Horse and Sitting Bull both will be there. Unless I change my plans, I should be back with you in August.*

I love you and wish you a Merry Christmas. (I'll bring you a beaver skin for a present and you can make a hat.)

Love,

John (Waukesha) Holcumb

John placed the letter in an envelope and put it away. He would go into Standing Rock when the weather broke and post it. Feeling better after finally writing his mother, he stepped outside the tipi to see the winter sun struggling through the clouds. Pulling his buffalo robe tightly around him, he walked through the hard snow toward Cedar Creek. He enjoyed the walk as he had spent too many days inside the smoky tipi. The creek was frozen solid. He picked up a few rocks and skipped them down the icy surface, enjoying the freedom of being outside again.

He finally returned to the village when the cold started creeping inside his clothing. As he approached Iron Hatchet's lodge, he saw two horses tied next to it. They looked familiar.

Could it be! he thought. He started running through the snow toward the lodge. Just then, the tipi flap flew back and a large white man stepped out.

"*Hoka Hey!*" John shouted, "It's Rusty."

Calf Woman and Chipeto took special care in preparing the meal that night. Since there was no fresh game available, dog meat was used. This meal was a special treat for the Dakotas, and, in the past, this custom had helped them survive many severe winters. The meal was finished when Iron Hatchet spoke.

"We are so pleased to see our friend Rusty again. Let us smoke the pipe together, as good friends should do. I have saved my best tobacco for just such an occasion. Calf Woman, bring my pipe."

The old woman dug through the bedding and found the tobacco bundle. Placing it before the chief, she moved back to her place behind her husband with Chipeto. Iron Hatchet opened the bundle and removed the pipe. Filling it with his prized tobacco, he lit it with a burning twig from the fire. Taking a deep draw, he slowly exhaled blue smoke, which twisted upwards through the hole in the top of the tipi. Then he passed the pipe to Rusty, who also puffed deeply.

The women prepared coffee, and soon all sat around sipping the hot liquid. Although John enjoyed the coffee and smoking, he was curious as to why Rusty had turned up at Cedar Creek.

"Tell us about your trapping, Rusty. Did you have trouble with the Crows? And why are you traveling in mid-winter?"

"Whoa," Rusty stopped him. "Just slow down a tad and I'll tell you all about it."

He drank again from his cup and resumed talking. "I traveled for many days from Iron Hatchet's camp up north until I finally found a little valley above the Yellowstone River. It mightn't have even been in Canada for all I know. Most damn beautiful place I ever saw—filled with beaver and deer and badger everywhere. Didn't have no trouble with the Crow, either. When I saw them on a couple occasions, I gave them some coffee and jerky, and they just mostly left me alone.

"I was really having a great season too. My traps was always full, as you can see by my furs over there on the floor. Really, almost a full season's work by mid-winter. Could've had my best year ever."

"Then why did you come back?" John asked.

"Well, one day about three weeks back, I was sitting in my *wick-iup*, trying to keep warm when I heard a rider approaching my camp. Taking my rifle with me, I stepped outside. To my surprise, it was a Sioux, not a Crow. We shared coffee and I found out his mission. He had been sent out by the Sioux agent to find all the Indians living off reservations to tell them that they had to report to their reservations by the end of January, or the army would come and get them and make them come in."

"But this is the middle of the winter!" John shouted. "No tribe could make such a trip at this time and survive."

"That's true," Rusty agreed. "This Sioux runner had already found Sitting Bull's tribe up by the Powder River country."

"And what did Sitting Bull tell him?" Iron Hatchet asked.

"Sitting Bull told him to tell the agent he would come in but not until the Moon of the New Grasses. The Sioux told me all the tribes he contacted were answering the same. After some more coffee, he rode off to return to his reservation.

"I left the next day to try and find your band, Chief. Traveling through this snow was just about the hardest trip I ever made. Damn near froze to death, but I didn't know if you had heard or not and I kind of feel responsible for young John here. I ain't telling you to go into the reservation, but you can bet there's going to be trouble come this spring if you don't.

"I just thought you better know." Rusty poured himself some coffee and stood up to stretch.

"Thank you for the warning, White Hair," Iron Hatchet said. "I have heard of this order from other Dakotas, but I also will not move in the winter, even though Standing Rock agency is very close. When spring comes, I will not want to spend it on a dead reservation. I will join my free brothers up near the Greasy Grass, and, if trouble comes, it will come. Better to die a man than live on like a dog."

The chief moved his hand sharply in front of him to indicate the subject matter was closed. They could talk of other more pleasant things, but not of the U.S. Army's order to the free tribes. It was quiet inside the warm tipi for a few minutes as everyone stared at the small fire. John pulled his robe over him to fight off the chill brought on by Rusty's news.

Rusty stayed on with the Dakota tribe through the balance of the winter. He hadn't intended to, but the lodge was warm, the conversation good, and soon the Moon When the Snow Melts was upon them. It was midApril when he decided to leave for St. Joseph, Missouri. Some of his kin lived there and it was a good trading post for his furs. He walked with John along Cedar Creek on the day he was to leave.

71

Several moments passed in silence before he finally queried what he had wanted to ask since returning.

"How long you going to stay with the Sioux, Johnny Boy? You've been living like an Indian for almost a year now. Do you think you'll ever go back?"

"Oh, yes, I will go back and see my mother again soon. She will be so proud to see her son as a Hunkpapa brave, and I miss her. I plan on heading back east sometime this summer after the big tribal gathering up near the Rosebud. Even though I have seen Crazy Horse, Sitting Bull will be there and I wish to see him, too. Then I will have actually seen the greatest leaders of my father's people."

Rusty bent down and squinted into the water.

"Will that satisfy you? I mean, will you then know enough about your people so's you can go back home? I remember back on that train last spring you was awful confused. Are you straightened out now?"

"I wish I could say I was," John answered. "But, the truth is, I'm more confused than ever. I have known more excitement in this year here with the Dakotas than in all my years in Chicago. I feel like a real man now. But war with my white brothers grows closer all the time and then what will I do? I am neither red nor white but something in between.

"Yes, Rusty, I'm going back to Chicago in the summer, but then my plans are not complete. I can't picture myself just fading back into a normal white man's life in Chicago and I don't know if I can come back here and live like all the other Sioux either.

"What do you think I ought to do?"

The old man took off his hat and slowly wiped his arm across his forehead. He turned to his young friend and placed his bear-like hand on his shoulder. "I don't know that I can answer that for you," Rusty said softly.

"I just don't know. I believe this year here has been right good for you. It's let you see and learn things that no damn book in Chicago could have ever teached you. But each man must decide for himself the kind of life he's going to lead. There are good points to both the Indian and the white man's way of livin'. The best possible solution would be to take the good things from each and live like that.

"Course, there ain't no such a way of livin' that I know of. Closest thing to it would be a trapper like myself. Now, I'd be more than glad to have you join up with me if you'd ever decide to trap. You just keep that in the back of your head when this summer is over."

"Thank you, Rusty," John said. "That's something to think about. But how would I ever find you if I would want to join you? Next fall you may be clear up into Oregon country, or even Canada."

"That's a right good question," Rusty answered. He paused for a minute as he thought about this problem.

"I know how," he said. "I'll send a letter to your mama's address in Chicago for you before I light out this fall to trap. That way, if you get back to Chicago this summer, you'll know where abouts I'm headin'. I'll write you every summer so you don't have to make up your mind this first summer. You can give me your mother's address before I go."

The two friends stood silently together, watching the icy water in the creek rushing by.

"Thank you for your offer, Rusty. It is a choice I may have to make soon, but for this summer I will be a Dakota brave and live like one. I will see much more of these prairies that my people call home, and maybe that will fill my needs for all my life. I don't know, but perhaps I will after this summer. Thank you again."

"Been my pleasure," Rusty answered. "C'mon, we gotta get back so's I can be on my way east. I'm anxious to drink some good whiskey and see a pretty gal's face and get my fill of civilization."

The two men walked through the cedar trees toward the village and Rusty's waiting horses.

Chapter Six
LITTLE BIG HORN

A month had passed since Iron Hatchet's band departed from Cedar Creek and marched across the prairies to Rosebud country. Iron Hatchet never seriously considered moving his tribe onto the reservation. He was born free and wild and would die the same way. He did not believe that the order to surrender and report to the reservation was a serious threat to a Dakota living on his ancestral lands. Some white man living thousands of miles away would not order around the Hunkpapa chief.

On the journey to Montana, many Indians, who had gone into the reservations during the winter with their chiefs to stay until the warm months arrived, accompanied the tribe. The meeting of Sitting Bull, Crazy Horse, Gall, and Two Moons of the Cheyenne near the Rosebud River was common knowledge among the Indians, and they deserted the reservations in droves to join the wild chiefs. Excitement ran through the traveling village as it approached the Rosebud River country.

Arriving early in the Moon of Making Fat—June—Iron Hatchet learned from his scouts that the great conference was no longer camped on the Rosebud. Because the thousands of Indian ponies had eaten all the grass along the Rosebud River, the chiefs decided to move the encampment near the river called the Greasy Grass. This river was known to the white man as the Little Big Horn.

While the Indian village was camped on the Rosebud, Crazy Horse and the Oglalas had ridden to the south and fought with General Crook's army in Rosebud Canyon. Although the battle lasted all day, Crazy Horse did not let his warriors charge wildly like in the old days, but kept them hidden amongst the rocks and boulders. The Indians shot their bows and rifles down the canyon at the confused soldiers, who were used to a skirmish line in which their superior rifles would win the battle. When the sun rose the next day, the soldiers could be seen far off to the south in retreat. It was a great victory for Crazy Horse and the Sioux.

John, sitting on Panka, looked down the green valley at the awesome powwow. The Indian village stretched for three miles up the twisting river with the great pony herds everywhere, grazing all around the tipis and *wickiups*. A smoky haze hung over the valley from the many tipi fires. The valley floor seemed to be alive with Indians as warriors could be seen everywhere, talking and laughing while their wives cooked the noon meal. The Greasy Grass River was full of the naked bodies of children playing and splashing in its icy waters.

Within the valley, the lodges were clustered in circles in a very definite order. The Hunkpapas were first, at the entrance to the camp, for their name meant "At the Front End of the Circle". The order then was Blackfeet, Sans Arcs, Minneconjous, Oglalas, Brules, and, last, was the circle of Cheyenne lodges under Two Moons. There were over ten thousand Indians gathered together, nearly four thousand of them warriors. It thrilled John to be a part of this great Indian assembly.

They had seen Sitting Bull a number of times, and each time they were impressed. The Dakota holy man mostly sat by his fire and talked to his people about the ever-increasing threat of the *wasicun*.

One day after Iron Hatchet's camp was set up, John sat inside the tipi eating with Little Horse.

"Have you heard about Sitting Bull's vision yet, Waukesha?" Little horse asked. "It's all over the camp."

"No, I haven't. What did the great medicine chief dream this time?"

"Well, in his dream, Sitting Bull saw many soldiers falling into the Indian camp with their heads down and hats falling off."

"What do you think it means?" John interrupted.

"It can only mean war with the white man. There will be a great victory for the Sioux with many dead soldiers. Wakantanka is going to punish the whites for trying to force us on the reservations during the winter. Sitting Bull is the greatest holy man in the Dakota Nation and his dream will come true."

Sunlight flooded into the tipi as the flap opened and Iron Hatchet entered. He sat down next to the boys, taking a piece of meat from the steaming pot with his knife.

"Were you speaking of Sitting Bull's dream?" he asked Little Horse.

"Yes, Father, we were. Have you heard something new?"

"Only many rumors of the blue soldiers coming. They are supposed to be east of here but no scouts have seen them yet. Crazy Horse sends out many scouts, so we will not be taken by surprise."

Iron Hatchet finished speaking to his son and turned to John. "What will you do, John Waukesha, when the soldiers come? Will you be able to fight your mother's people? If the soldiers find you, you may have to fight them, for you surely look like any other Sioux warrior in the village. Perhaps it would be better if you went up into the Big Horn Mountains until the battle is over. The Great Spirit may come to you and help you decide your future while you are there."

John did not answer immediately, but thought over his uncle's words carefully before he spoke.

"I have thought much of this problem since we started here, Iron Hatchet, and my heart is very heavy. For though I love the Dakota people, I also love many white people. However, I am filled with anger for my white brother for what he is doing to the Dakotas. This land is Sioux and should always remain Sioux. Yet I was raised as a white, and I cannot turn my back on them. Some of my friends from Chicago might even be soldiers by now, and I would not want to fight them. Perhaps I should leave the village now so I do not bring shame to Iron Hatchet's lodge."

John sighed as he finished speaking.

The tipi was very quiet. None of the three Dakotas spoke until Iron Hatchet moved next to his nephew. "Do not leave for fear of bringing shame to us, John Waukesha, for you have proven yourself to be a man. You could never disgrace us." His voice grew louder.

"I am as proud of you as my own son, Little Horse, and you will stay with us until your heart tells you to return to Chicago. When the soldiers come, I will send you out to scout far from the village where there is no fighting. When the fighting is done, you may return to us and share in the glory, as no man should have to fight his brother. I have spoken."

Iron Hatchet stood up and walked out of the tipi, closing the flap behind him to shroud the two youths in darkness. Moments passed in silence until John spoke to his cousin.

"Will it be cowardly to leave the village if a fight starts, Little Horse? Speak the truth with me *hohe*, my brother."

"To fight one's brother would be a cowardly thing," Little Horse answered. "I could never fight you, so I understand how it is. Do as Iron Hatchet says and you will not be a coward. Anyway, perhaps the blue soldiers will be fought far away from the village and you won't be faced with the problem. Come; let's go swimming in the Greasy Grass. The cool water will help us forget about the white man and perhaps some young girls will be there to watch us."

Hunting and swimming filled most of the days that followed. John tried to enjoy the carefree life of the Indian camp, but the constant talk of war bothered him. Iron Hatchet and Little Horse were preparing for a battle, and he was left out of the plans.

Once again he was in the middle.

A week passed and he finally decided to leave the great Sioux encampment and return to Chicago to seek his mother's advice. She had always guided him in the past and she would again. Then, there was always the possibility of hooking up with Rusty. Later, he might even return to the Dakotas, but now he needed someone to talk to about all that had happened to him. He sat inside Iron Hatchet's lodge preparing to face his uncle with his decision. It would be hard to leave his Dakota brothers, but he was sure they would see each other again someday.

Suddenly there was shouting outside.

"Soldiers! The soldiers are here!"

John ran from the tipi and looked toward the river where, unbelievably, U.S. Army soldiers charged the Hunkpapa village. The cavalry rode in formation with their horses lined up neatly as they crossed the stream. The soldiers fired their rifles wildly, shooting into the village.

They must be crazy, John thought. There were fewer than one hundred and fifty blue-coated soldiers riding across the river to attack the village of ten thousand Indians. The camp came alive with movement as the warriors grabbed their rifles and bows and ran down toward the soldiers.

"Take the women and children up toward the Cheyenne camp," a warrior shouted as he ran past John. "They must be protected." The brave disappeared into the dust and confusion of the fighting. Shots were being fired rapidly now and the bullets were whizzing into the village. John walked swiftly through the tipis away from the fighting, but the women were already hustling away from the camp up the river. Some small children cried, but most walked quickly and unafraid, following their brothers and sisters.

He returned to the village edge and could see the soldiers had dismounted; they were fighting their way back into the timber stand near the Little Big Horn. The Sioux swarmed around the soldiers, shouting and yelling, beating back the troopers. Firing from behind trees and the high grasses, the Indians tried to encircle the blue coats so there would be no escaping.

The turmoil stunned John as he watched his white brothers fighting his red brothers. He felt panic welling up within him. His worst dreams had come true. Stumbling alongside his tipi, a Sioux warrior on a yellow horse rode past him. John looked up at the brave and he knew it was Crazy Horse by the red hawk in his hair and the lighting streaks on his face.

"*Hoka Hey,*" Crazy Horse shouted to his followers. "It is a fine day to die. Fight together and we shall have a great victory."

Kicking his warhorse, he rode down toward the timber stand where the army troopers were taking up their defense. The Dakotas appeared to be winning the battle with many soldiers dead on the grass. Wounded horses whinnied in pain, struggling to stand but falling back again. The air smelled strong of gun smoke, the loud crack of rifles still coming up to the village from the river's edge.

Iron Hatchet rode up the valley toward John, carrying a new soldier's rifle in his hand. Stopping next to John, he dropped from his pony and spoke breathlessly.

"The battle goes well for the Dakota today, my son. We shall soon kill all of these soldiers in the woods. *Hoka Hey! Ho Ho!* United we can defeat the whites. All Indians must be brothers. We shall be unbeatable and these lands will always be ours."

The old chief could hardly contain his excitement. He turned back toward the battlefield where the gunfire was decreasing.

"I must go back before it is over," he said. "I know these are hard times for you. Go far above the Cheyenne camp and make sure there are no more soldiers at the other end of the village. Scout well."

Iron Hatchet was shouting his instructions so the other braves would know why John was leaving the battleground. Then he bent over and whispered.

"Do not return until the sun is down, as the dead blue soldiers will not be treated well. The Cheyenne have many widows caused by

Long Hair's army at the Washita, and these women will not let the soldiers enter the happy hunting ground with all their parts."

John understood the words of his uncle. The bodies would be mutilated. "Thank you, Uncle," he said. "I am grateful to you."

Mounting Panka, John raced through the village, moving north along the Greasy Grass River. The villages were all deserted—the women and children had gone out on the plains with the ponies for safety, and the young men were trying to kill the hated white soldiers. He slowed Panka to a walk and swung his pony across the stream, heading up to the ridges above the Little Big Horn Valley. He and Panka climbed steadily until the entire valley stretched out below them, the river winding crazily toward the Yellowstone.

"Are you tiring, Panka?" John asked his pony. "It has been a hard ride. We'll stop over by the ridge and you can eat grass there while I try to straighten out my thoughts."

Dismounted, John stroked Panka, and then shooting erupted somewhere in the valley below. He knew it was too close for it to be the fighting from the Hunkpapa village. The firing suddenly grew in intensity as he crawled up the ridge and cautiously looked down below him.

The valley was once again alive with soldiers and Indians battling. The blue coats had formed a stand on a slight knoll, but the woods around them were alive with Sioux and Cheyenne. Smoke and gunfire were everywhere as the Indians fired at the exposed cavalrymen, killing men and horses both. Riding in an ever-smaller circle, the Sioux advanced toward the soldiers.

John could not hear the agonizing screams of dying men. Only the rifle shots could be heard as the smoke floated up in puffs. Some of the soldiers tried to crawl off through the woods but were found and killed by the Dakotas and Cheyenne. As the battle went on, the remaining soldiers began to run out of ammunition and the gunfire slowed down. The Indians swarmed over the last defenders, killing them all. None escaped as the Indians searched the culverts and ditches for any wounded. Waukesha saw them find one wounded cavalry-man and the five warriors pumped many arrows into him, long after he was dead. Such was the hatred of the Indians that day for the blue soldiers. They scalped most of the corpses, and stripped off their blue jackets as victory souvenirs.

Gall and Crazy Horse suddenly appeared, and, signaling the warriors, they rode off toward the camp and the other soldiers still down by the Hunkpapas. John watched in dismay as the Indian women hurried up the knoll and began stripping the dead soldiers. John felt his stomach churning as the women used their knives on the dead bodies, cutting and slashing so the soldiers would be deformed in the next world. John could watch no longer and he turned away, sliding down the hill. The whole scene was all a nightmare to him. Perhaps his adopted mother, Calf Woman, was down there with the others.

The hatred, he thought. *The hatred between my peoples is so great. What can I do? How can this killing be stopped?*

He sat up and, leaning against a tree, vomited violently. All the sick feeling he had been holding gushed from his insides in a torrent of release. Finally, he stopped and crawled back up the hill and looked below again.

All was still except for the buzzards slowly circling above in the clear blue sky. The Little Big Horn valley was quiet and looked normal except for the unnatural glare of the sun reflecting off dead white bodies. About one hundred and fifty bodies were spread over the knoll alongside dead horses, with more hidden in the underbrush.

"It is not a pretty sight, is it, John Waukesha?"

John heard the familiar voice behind him and turned quickly to see Iron Hatchet standing below him. The old chief was dressed in his full ceremonial splendor.

Iron Hatchet was not a handsome man. His nose was large, very pointed, and his chin protruded too far. Still, he looked like a magnificent chief dressed in his eagle feather war bonnet with the white feathers running down his back to the ground. He was wearing a deerskin shirt over cotton trousers; both beaded in blue and yellow.

"Why are you here, Iron Hatchet?" John asked. "I thought you would be in the camp celebrating this victory."

"I am going there when I have finished speaking with you," the Dakota chief answered quietly.

"For this has been a great victory today for our people and we should celebrate. It has pleased the Great Spirit that we won. All of Sitting Bull's dreams have come true: the soldiers fell into our camp and are dead. But because I have grown to love you as my own, I had to come and speak with you, for this victory over the whites has surely upset you.

"Yes it has, Father."

"I knew it would. I wish I could say it was the last battle between our peoples, but it will not be. The *wasicun* will not be happy until all the Indians are dead or on reservations. This defeat will only make the White Father in Washington very mad, who will send many more troops into Sioux lands, and we will have to fight them. We do have to fight for our lands, John Waukesha; they are all we have left. Do you understand that?"

"Yes I do, Iron Hatchet. I believe the Dakota people belong here and must fight if necessary, but the sight of so much killing had made me sick."

"As it should. Before the white man came, our fighting did not kill many men. A few died but counting coup was usually enough for us. Now the whites have come and war has become strictly killing. I never saw a people so good at killing as the white man is, for he has invented more ways to kill than all the Indian tribes have in all our days. War is no longer a way to prove one's bravery, but only for killing. We are forced to kill the white man when he tries to take our lands, and, in that way, he has made us like him, I am sad to say. But, my son, if they would only stop coming, stop attacking our villages, stop killing our women and babies, then all the killing would stop. We are not to blame for today. They attacked our village on our lands, so we had to finish it for them. Try to remember that in the days ahead."

The chief finished his speech and walked up the hill next to John. Putting his arm around the youth's shoulders, he led him down to their ponies.

"Get up on Panka," he said to John, "and ride north until sundown. That will put you near a rock formation, the whites call Squaw's Head. You will easily see why it is called that. Camp there until we join you tomorrow, for I am taking my tribe north away from this place. Soon there will be more soldiers and we have no bullets left to fight them with now."

"But where will we go?" John asked.

"Into Canada, I think. To the land of the Grandmother, where it will be safe for a while. Go now, I will see you in the morning."

"Thank you, Iron Hatchet. I think I will stay with the Sioux awhile longer." After climbing on Panka, he kicked her gently and they trotted up the trail to Squaw's Head.

The sun was dipping low beyond the Montana hills when John saw the rock formation protruding from the flat valley in the distance. The shadows were long, and the young brave was weary as his pony walked slowly up the valley. It was quiet now, only the red-winged black birds squawked at him as he rode passed them. A rabbit jumped up in front of Panka, scurrying into the underbrush, a flash of white against the green. The sudden movement startled John.

"I have been daydreaming, Panka," he said. "I had better stay alert in case there are more soldiers around. I don't think they will ask me if I'm part white before they start shooting."

The campsite he selected was on the east side of Squaw's Head, so the first light would wake him. Cutting down willow branches from the nearby creek, he built a *wickiup* and lined the floor with a bed of pine needles. Satisfied with his work, he tied Panka in a small willow stand, taking his bow and arrows with him. Patting Panka, he talked to his pony. "Perhaps that rabbit we saw is still close by Panka. With some luck, I will return soon with my supper. I have not eaten since this morning's sunrise, so long ago."

Running quietly along the stream, he stopped at a place where the creek opened up to form a small pool. Walking away from the water's edge, he lay down in the high grass to wait. He was sure that some animals would soon be coming to drink and he would be ready. As the sun dropped slowly below the hills, the forest around the stream grew dark. John squinted, trying to spot some movement near the water's edge. At last a rabbit hopped into view, and sat eating on the greens growing near the stream. John aimed true and let the arrow fly, killing the cottontail instantly.

John jumped up and shouted in elation. He started to run toward his kill, when a slight movement behind a cottonwood caught his eye. He instinctively dove for the ground as a rifle shot cracked out, and the bullet tore into the dirt behind him. Crawling frantically for a large log, he slid behind it as another shot slammed into the log. His breath coming in hard gasps, Waukesha fought down the panic pushing through him. Now was the time to be calm and act like a Dakota warrior, not a young white boy. He hadn't seen his attacker very well but he knew the man was wearing a blue cavalry coat. Something was strange about him, but John had not gotten a good look at him. Thinking about his situation, John knew he was in serious trouble. He had only a bow and arrow against a rifle. Luckily, his enemy was not a good a shot or he would be dead by now.

Another shot rang out, chewing up the dirt by John's face. Soon the attacker would move in on him and that would be his end unless he acted quickly. Crawling the length of the rotting log, he slid down a culvert at its end into a small creek bed. The rocks tore at his bare knees as be bellied up the stream toward a stand of young trees. He crept into the trees and slid an arrow into his bow. Raising his head above the creek bank, he was looking at the cottonwoods where his attacker should have been, but he was not there.

John rolled over the culvert's edge and lay still in the high weeds. Scanning the forest, he could not see his enemy. The fading sunlight cast strange shadows and several times he thought he saw his ambusher, only to find out it was a tree limb or rock formation.

The minutes passed by agonizingly slow. John was tense, watching and listening. A twig snapped behind and above him. He turned. In the trees stood a Ree, a Custer Indian Scout, wearing the blue coat of the Union Army. John shot his arrow at the Ree's chest just as the scout's rifle fired. The bullet tore into John's side, burning through the muscle above his hip. He was knocked back and rolled in pain as he grabbed his bleeding side.

I will die like a man, he thought, as he waited for the Ree to come and kill him. Pushing with his right arm, he rolled over on his back, but the Army Scout was not standing above him. John looked into the trees, but he was not there.

Dragging himself slowly up the rise, he discovered why he had not been finished off. The Ree lay dead against the tree where he had fallen, John's arrow stuck through his neck. The Indian's eyes were still open as if in surprise, his rifle lying across his lap.

"My God," John muttered. "What a lucky shot. The Great Spirit smiled on me this day.

"I am sorry, brother," he said to the dead Indian, "but you left me no choice. It was either kill or be killed, much like the Sioux and the whites today. We kill each other without even knowing why."

Taking his bow, he counted coup on the dead Ree. He was surprised that he didn't feel remorse over the killing, but was actually feeling quite proud. He had slain the worst kind of Sioux enemy—a man who sold out his people for the white man's pay. All the Sioux hated the Indian Scouts even more than the white soldiers.

Strange, he thought, *that I should actually be proud of this deed. I guess I am more Dakota than I thought.*

The pain in his side was throbbing hard now and he pressed against the wound to stop the bleeding. He had to get back to his camp and rest, but first he removed the blue shirt from the dead brave and took the Ree's Winchester rifle.

"Don't worry," he said. "I will leave your hair, but you won't need your gun anymore. I will. May your journey to the Happy Hunting Grounds be short."

Waukesha closed the brave's eyes and struggled to his feet. He took a few cautious steps and, using the rifle as a crutch, limped through the trees and onto the flat prairie. The sun was down when he reached his camp, where he fell into his *wickiup*. John rolled on his back and passed out.

Chapter Seven

CANADIAN EXILES

Iron Hatchet's Hunkpapas broke camp early on the morning of June 26, 1876, and the entire village was heading north by mid-morning. It would take the slow moving camp many hours to reach Squaw's Head, so Little Horse rode Swift Moon ahead to scout the ridges for any blue soldiers that might be in the area. On his head was a cavalry hat, a battle souvenir from the Little Big Horn. An eagle feather was stuck in it, for he had proven his manhood by slaying a trooper near the Hunkpapa village during the first attack. The soldier had fallen off his horse as he attempted to climb the steep muddy bank of the Little Big Horn, seeking the safety of the hills above the river. While the trooper struggled to escape the swift flowing stream, Little Horse and several other braves fired their arrows into him. At least three hit the trooper and he fell face down into the stream.

Ignoring the gunfire and danger, Little Horse had leapt into the river, kicking the water high as he ran. He reached the dead soldier while bullets splashed the water all around him. As Little Horse counted coup on the trooper with his bow, he took off the soldier's hat and scalped the fallen enemy, dropping the body back into the water. Bullets danced in the water near him, but Little Horse was not hit, for his magic was strong. It had been a brave deed, the kind to be retold many times over the years.

Little Horse was recalling yesterday's battle as he rode to the summit approaching the Squaw's Head valley. What a tale he would have to tell his brother, John Waukesha. He looked up the flat prairie toward the rock formation known as Squaw's Head. She eternally looked east to greet the sun each morning.

Squinting into the sunlight, he tried to find the smoke from John's fire, but there was no movement near the rocks. Little Horse scanned the entire valley, from the mountains on the left, past the woman, and to the creek on the right. Then he saw them. Circling above the cottonwood trees growing near the creek were buzzards, slowly gliding on the mountain breezes. Kicking Swift Moon hard, he shouted to his pony and they galloped down the slope.

"Hurry, Swift Moon. My brother may be hurt and need my help. Hurry. Fly like the North Wind. Faster. *Hopo*."

His heart pounded wildly as they approached the stand of trees. The screeching buzzards greeted him. Entering the woods, he saw a dead body against a tree.

"Aii, I am too late," he muttered as he dismounted and ran into the trees. His anguish quickly disappeared as he saw it was not John Waukesha, but a Ree, clad in blue soldier's pants. Little Horse bent over the body and saw the arrow in his neck.

It has Waukesha's markings on it, he thought. *My brother has killed an Army scout, but I wonder if the Ree has killed Waukesha.*

He searched the creek area, finding only a dead rabbit, also killed by John Waukesha's arrow. The Dakota brave then found a spot with much dried blood, and he knew John was wounded. John's trail led through the trees toward Squaw's Head. Little Horse stopped next to the Ree and quickly took his scalp.

"John Waukesha could not bring himself to do that Ree dog," he said, "but a low-dog soldier scout does not deserve to keep his hair. You probably tried to kill my brother from the bushes by shooting him in the back. Now you must enter the Spirit World without your braids."

He ran through the trees, climbed on Swift Moon, and quickly picked up John's trail. It was easy tracking as John had stumbled repeatedly during his struggle back to his *wickiup*, leaving the grass stained crimson. Little Horse feared John had been mortally wounded. When he reached his cousin's *wickiup*, he found Waukesha lying on the ground, covered with sweat and moaning in pain. Little Horse placed the Ree's blue coat under John's head, and wiped the sweat from his face. The wound had stopped bleeding, the blood caked dry on John's side.

"Rest easy, *Hohe*, my brother," Little Horse said. "It is me, Little Horse.

"You will be all right now. Iron Hatchet will soon be here, and Calf Woman will care for you. When you are better, you must tell me how you came to slay the Ree. Now you must rest."

Recognizing his cousin's voice, John opened his eyes. Little Horse was smiling at him, wearing a trooper's hat on his head.

"Ohh, Little Horse," he mumbled. "I did not think we would meet again in this world. I had to kill an Indian scout who ambushed me but—"

John stopped talking a minute to catch his breath. He was having trouble getting his thoughts straight.

"But now he is dead."

"*Hoka Hey!*" Little Horse exclaimed. "He is dead alright. I found him down by the stream with the mighty Waukesha's arrow in his neck. When did you kill him?"

"Last night at sundown. I was hunting for game when he attacked me. If he were a better shot, I would be dead by now, but Wakantanka smiled on me, and I am still alive. I don't believe my wound will kill me as the bullet left my body."

"I do not think it too serious either, but, for now, you should be resting. Lay your head back, and, when you wake, Calf Woman will be here. Sleep now while I light the fire."

John closed his eyes and immediately drifted away, his strength sapped. John dreamed of many things in his delirium. Chicago and his mother appeared and then she was chased off by a thundering herd of buffalo, followed by John riding on Panka. The dust from the herd faded away and he was back home again, helping his mother. He stoked the potbellied stove as his mother warmed herself in her rocker, her face reflecting the contentment she felt at having her son home. He hadn't realized how much he missed her.

"Mother, Mother," he called out. "I'm coming home soon. Don't worry."

"I am here, John Waukesha," a woman's voice answered him. "Rest easy and we will take care of you."

John struggled back to reality and opened his eyes to see he was inside a tipi, lying on a pine needle bed. The voice he heard belonged to Calf Woman, who was wiping the sweat from his face with a cool wet cloth.

"Do not worry, John Waukesha. I am here to make you better. The bullet only left a mark like a bad rope burn, and will heal quickly. Chipeto makes soup for you and we will have you at your full strength soon. We have nursed many braves back to health who were worse off than you."

John relaxed and enjoyed the cool feeling as Calf Woman continued dabbing his face. He could see Chipeto stirring the iron kettle over the fire. A young woman, who sat next to Chipeto on a buffalo robe, cried, the tears running down her cheeks as her body shook with each sob. She was young, perhaps seventeen or eighteen summers, and wore a plain buckskin dress with fur tied around her braids.

"Who is that beautiful young girl?" he whispered to Calf Woman. "And why is she crying?"

"That is Wakala, the widow of Three Fingers."

"The widow of Three Fingers?" John asked in amazement. "What happened to Three Fingers? I saw him only two days ago."

"He was killed by the blue coats down by the Greasy Grass. He was shot in the timber battle, but we got his body back and gave him a full warrior's funeral. Now he is in the next world living as a Dakota warrior."

Chipeto joined the conversation.

"That is so, John Waukesha. Three Fingers was a real man. Why, he killed three of the white soldiers after he was shot in the chest. Such a warrior. His belt was full of the scalps of the Crows. It was a bullet that bounced off a large rock that struck him down in his prime, leaving this young girl with no husband to care for her."

"She will have a hard time finding another man as good as Three Fingers," Calf Woman added.

"I did not even know that Three Fingers was married," John said. "I always remember him sitting alone at his lodge. I thought his wife died many winters past."

"His first wife died long ago. He only married this girl at the great Sioux encampment by the Rosebud."

"She was the only daughter of Mokala, an old friend of Iron Hatchet," Chipeto elaborated. "When Mokala died, Iron Hatchet arranged the marriage. It was a good solution for both Wakala and Three Fingers."

John listened intently as the two women continued their story, obviously delighted in having such a captive audience for their tale.

"They were married by the Rosebud when all the tribes came together," Calf Woman continued. "For her tribe is Hunkpapa but of another clan. They camped near the Powder River with Sitting Bull during the last winter. Three Fingers paid many fine ponies for her and he got a bargain at that, for she is as gentle as the doe and very obedient. She also sews well and does excellent bead work for being so young."

Chipeto interrupted again.

"And now she has nothing left, no one to keep her. It has been a sad spring. She has lost her father and husband, and so she sits and cries. She will stay in our lodge; Iron Hatchet will provide for her because he made the marriage arrangements, obliged to do so. Any Hunkpapa would do the same. We will treat her as if she were our own sister."

"I see," said John, resting his tired head on a blanket. "Thank you both for caring for me. Tell Wakala my heart is heavy for her."

He closed his eyes and, after the two women covered him with a buffalo robe, they crawled over to the fire and resumed cooking. John snuck a look across the tipi at the young woman. She had stopped crying. She looked very beautiful to John, as she sat staring into the fire. Shutting his eyes again, he drifted into sleep with the image of a pretty young girl on his mind.

A firm hand shook his shoulder and woke him. Opening his eyes, he looked up into Iron Hatchet's face.

"How are you feeling, my son?" the old man asked him gently. "You gave Little Horse quite a scare when he found you sleeping in your *wickiup*."

"I am feeling better today."

"That is good, for we should start our journey to Canada today. We have stayed here for one full day, so you should be strong enough to travel with us. I do not wish to stay close to the Greasy Grass much longer. We have no ammunition for our guns, and the blue coats may come back."

"I can travel," John said. "I will need some help getting up on Panka, but I can surely ride."

"Not so quickly," the chief answered. "You will ride the *travois* today and perhaps tomorrow you may try your pony.

"You have again proven yourself to be a true Dakota. Because of your brave deeds, I am sure your father is smiling down on us."

The chief disappeared through the flap into the dazzling daylight. John's heart filled with pride at his uncle's words.

The women of the tribe quickly dismantled the camp, dropping the tipis and tying them together for the trip. After Little Horse helped John onto the *travois*, he covered him with a blanket and tied him in with rawhide straps.

"You look like a large *papoose*," Little Horse laughed.

"I feel worse than that."

"Don't feel so badly, Waukesha. I have something for you that I took from the Ree you killed."

Little Horse handed him the Ree's Remington rifle. Tied to it was the scalp of the dead man.

"Take it," Little Horse insisted. "You have earned it. Our people believe it is a just thing to do, so you must keep it. The Ree are all mongrel dogs that deserve to die. Keep it."

"I will take it, as you wish, but I do not think I can ever scalp a man. I will keep this scalp because you are my brother, and wish me to keep it. I do it to honor you."

John laid the rifle across his lap, the black scalp hanging near the ground.

As the camp started its journey north, John found the ride on the *travois* unbelievably rough. The poles dug in the dirt, dropping into ruts and jolting him constantly, while dust from the ponies blew into his face. The coughing from the dust tore at his side, causing him much pain.

The next day, John rode Panka. As a self-respecting brave, he would not ride on the *travois* again. He had eaten enough dust to last him for a lifetime.

The journey to the Land of the Grandmother took about a month. Most of the women and children walked while the braves rode their ponies, scouting constantly for the blue coats. The Indians were not anxious for another fight, and twice they changed direction to miss the soldiers.

John's strength increased daily and by the sixth day he felt little pain from his bullet wound. Calf Woman and Chipeto had made sure that no infection started, and the stiffness was leaving. He wore the Ree's blue coat as he rode with Little Horse. They both were proud of their war souvenirs: soldier's hats and jackets, and the hair of two dead men. It was like the first summer for them as they hunted the woods, fished the streams, and raced their ponies while the clan slowly moved north.

The tribe entered Canada in late July and settled in Saskatchewan Territory on the shores of Old Wives Lake. They were greeted as brothers by the Blackfeet Sioux who lived there permanently, and offered whatever food supplies the Blackfeet had. They set up their camp close to the Blackfeet village, which was a large one of about five hundred people. The Blackfeet were fierce warriors, destroyers of many Crow and Albisone Indians in their fighting days, but now they had touched pen to paper with the government of the Grandmother and vowed to fight no more with their red brothers. The Canadian government supplied them with weapons, blankets, and rations in return for the Blackfeet keeping the peace. The Canadian Mounted Police dealt with raids on the white settler's cattle or ranches promptly and severely. The Canadian courts handled any crimes involving whites and Indians according to treaty.

John's wound was almost healed by the time they arrived in Canada. The Hunkpapa camp was quickly set up and life slowly returned to normal in the village.

Several weeks had flown by when John Waukesha and Little Horse disappeared into the pine forest to hunt. They walked along the sandy shores of Old Wives Lake, the afternoon sun reflecting brightly off the crystal clear waters. The sunlight danced in their eyes as they squinted to see across the lake. The air felt clear and cool, and the young men were silent as they walked. It felt great to be alive, free, and in no danger of attack from the United States cavalry. They walked through the shadowy trees for over an hour, seeing no game, but not feeling disappointed. It was pleasant just being in Wakantanka's forest with his trees, lake, and cloudless sky.

Sitting down on two large, gray rocks near the water's edge, they lazily skipped stones across the lake.

As they watched, a large hawk circled slowly far out over the lake, swooping down occasionally and skimming along the water to touch it with his talons. But the hawk caught no fish while they watched, and soon disappeared into the green hills on the far shore of the lake.

"It is beautiful here," John said quietly to Little Horse. "The Great Spirit has made this spot very special."

"Yes, he has," Little Horse answered. "I can see why our Blackfeet brothers have settled here. All of the Great One's creatures live in harmony here. Maybe my father will keep us in Canada for many seasons."

They fell silent again; only the lapping noise of the waves could be heard. Occasionally, a hawk's screech would carry over the lake, but it was not unpleasant to them.

"How many summers have you seen?" Little Horse asked.

"I'm eighteen. Why do you ask? You know I am very near to you in years."

"Yes, I know, but I have seen the way you look at Wakala and it is the look of a man, not a boy. Perhaps you will want her for your wife before much longer."

John looked at his friend in disbelief. "The way I look at Wakala" he exclaimed. "Ha, I have seen you look at her, as though she were a baby fawn. Do not talk like I am love-struck, for surely you have thought of her as your wife. Do you deny this is so?"

Little Horse thought over his cousin's words. "Perhaps you also speak the truth. She is as beautiful as any woman I have ever seen. But, I thought of her as a wife for you, not for me. That is the truth."

"And I thought of her as a wife for you. I did not intend to take a Dakota wife, for I don't know my future plans. What if I return to Chicago? How would she be treated back there? No, there are too many problems for me."

"There are often solutions for such problems," Little Horse said to him. "I believe you are seriously thinking of her as a wife, no matter what your tongue says. Your heart will decide this matter, not your mind. However it turns out my brother, it will not come between us. Our bond is above jealousy. She will make a fine wife for either one of us, and the loser will still be the winner's friend and brother."

Little Horse finished speaking and clasped his cousin's hand firmly. They smiled at each other and, turning, they walked back toward their village.

As evening fell over the Hunkpapa camp, the tipi fires were lit early against the unusually cool August winds. The fire's warm glow lit up Iron Hatchet's lodge while the women busied themselves, unpacking and making new pine needle beds. Calf Woman and Chipeto chattered constantly with Wakala while the three braves sat silently smoking. Both John and Little Horse tried to watch Wakala without being seen by the other while she sewed a robe, the buffalo bone needle working swiftly through the hide. Her hands gracefully moved back and forth as she deliberately avoided the stares of the two young men.

Iron Hatchet sat drinking his coffee, watching the two braves. He knew that they both were anxious to please Wakala, and perhaps eventually marry her. After all, she had been married only two weeks to Three Fingers and her mourning period was over. She was a beautiful young woman and needed a young man for a husband. Iron Hatchet would not interfere in their competition for her. It was the way of the Sioux to vie for a young woman's hand, the best man winning. The loser was not held in disgrace, but would soon be back at another maiden's lodge trying for her hand. It had been like this for many generations. Of course, the parents, for political or financial reasons, arranged some marriages, but Iron Hatchet had won Calf Woman from many other braves, and he considered it a real test for a young man. The old chief reached over and tapped John Waukesha on the shoulder.

"Yes, Father?" John said, turning. "Did you wish to speak with me?"

"I do, my son. Come outside and walk with me so we may talk alone. We will not be gone long, Little Horse."

They walked down the slope of the shore under an incredibly clear night, millions of stars shining brightly in the black heavens above. It was very quiet, with the wind barely stirring the lake.

"It is a beautiful night," John said. "In Chicago we could not see most of the stars because of the smoke from houses and factories. You can almost see God in these beautiful skies."

"Do you think often of Chicago these days?" Iron Hatchet asked.

"Not of the city. Only of my mother. I have not seen her for two summers now and I worry about her. Other than for her, I have no desire to return to Chicago and its crowded wooden houses, its smoke-filled skies. On nights like these, I don't think I'll ever go back there, and I'll remain a Dakota like my father.

"That is music as sweet as a whippoorwill's song to my ears, John Waukesha," Iron Hatchet said. "I wish you to stay with us always. Your father would be pleased. Do you still carry his medicine bag?"

"Always. I would not be without it. It is my magic."

"And great magic it is," Iron Hatchet said, reaching inside his buckskin shirt.

"Here is something to add to it, something that is your own magic. It is the foot of the rabbit you killed near the Squaw's Head creek. It's magic helped you slay our age-old enemy and bring further glory to the lodge of Iron Hatchet. Little Horse returned to the creek to bring it back for you."

"Thank you. I will put it in my father's medicine bag and make my magic stronger than ever."

They had now walked the sandy lakeshore far from the lights of the Hunkpapa village; the tipi fires were barely visible through the buffalo hides. Sitting on a large rock, Iron Hatchet removed his moccasins and plunged his feet into the icy waters.

"I have another matter to discuss with you," the old man continued. He let his feet soak in the water. "I believe your heart feels much love toward the young widow Wakala. Is this true or not?"

"I am not sure, Iron Hatchet. She is the most beautiful girl I have ever seen, and, yet, I hesitate to think of her as a possible wife for me. I still plan on returning to Chicago before deciding my future plans. Besides, I do not know the Dakota style of courting, and fear to make a fool of myself."

"I cannot solve your first problem, that is up to you. But as far as courting goes, it is very simple. You must only convince the young widow of your love, and win her from Little Horse. Normally, the young man offers horses to the bride's father, but she has none, and I will not accept any ponies from my sons. Although I am her protector now, I would not feel right in accepting such a gift. She will be free to choose whichever one she wants, and I will not interfere. If your heart wins over your head and you decide to try to marry her, I will help guide you, so your chances are at least as good as Little Horse's. From then on, it is out of my hands."

The old chief put his hand on John's shoulder and squeezed it firmly. Reaching inside his shirt again, he pulled out another object that John could not make out in the dark.

"Take this," Iron Hatchet said as he handed the object to John. "It is a flute made for me by a medicine man when I was courting Calf Woman many summers ago. It has big magic and will help win the heart of Wakala, if you decide to court her. Take it and I will leave you to think on this awhile. I will not try to change your mind once it is set."

As he stood up to leave, Iron Hatchet looked up at the heavens.

"The Great Wakantanka will guide you. Do not worry," he said, and walked off barefoot into the darkness of the wooded shore.

John held the flute up to the sky, trying to see its form more clearly. It was carved into the shape of a bird's head, with five holes in the top, and he could barely make out that it was painted blue and yellow. He placed it to his mouth and blew, moving his fingers very slowly to learn the sounds the instrument made. It had a beautiful tone, blending with the night noises as it carried over the lake. Waukesha had heard skilled Sioux play this instrument beautifully, but his own simple song sounded pleasant to him. As he walked through the trees toward the camp, he slipped the flute inside his shirt. He would need much more practice before trying it in front of his friends.

The village stirred as John walked into its center. He found several strange horses tied up near Iron Hatchet's lodge, and a large crowd was trying to see inside. John pushed through the crowd into the tipi to find two Royal Canadian Mounted Policemen seated around the fire. They were trying to talk to Iron Hatchet in English, but were not having much luck. The old chief kept repeating "Coffee, coffee" to all of their questions, thinking some sort of trading was going on.

"Why does Iron Hatchet bring his Sioux people to the land of the Grandmother?" the Sergeant asked.

"Coffee, coffee," Iron Hatchet answered, smiling broadly at the white man.

"It's no use, Sergeant," the other man said to his friend. "We'll have to go up to the Blackfeet camp and get the interpreter. We could go on all night like this."

"No need to do that," John broke into the conversation, speaking in English for the first time in several months. His voice sounded strange in his old language. "I can speak English and will act as interpreter for Iron Hatchet."

"Ahh, that's good," the sergeant said with a smile. "It will greatly simplify matters. What are you called?"

"Waukesha," John answered, volunteering no further information.

"Good, Waukesha. I'm Sergeant Burton and this is Corporal Hall. We are here representing her Majesty Queen Victoria's Canadian Government, and we need to find out some information on Iron Hatchet's tribe for our reports. He has never brought his people here before, so we need some facts. Can you understand all that I've just told you?"

"Yes, I can understand."

"You speak English remarkably well, Waukesha," Burton said. "Tell me, are you Iron Hatchet's son?"

"Only by adoption. He is really my uncle. My father is gone onto the Spirit World. My uncle took care of me, as he takes care of all his people."

"That's getting me back to the point, Waukesha," the Mountie said. "Why has he brought his people to Canada? Where do you come from originally?"

"They want to know why we are here, and where we came from. What do you wish for me to tell them?" John asked Iron Hatchet.

Iron Hatchet looked at the two Mounties momentarily and then back to John. "Tell them we are a peace-loving tribe from down near Sand Creek in the Dakotas, but do not tell them the true reason why we are here. They will soon hear of the U.S. Army's defeat by the Greasy Grass River and, being *wasicun,* they might become angry with us. Tell them whatever you like, but make it a good story. You are half-white and will know what they like to hear. And somehow manage to get us some more coffee."

Iron Hatchet stood up and put his arm around Waukesha to show that this youth was speaking for him. He turned to the Mounties who were still sitting, and proclaimed very loudly for all to hear.

"Coffee," and he sat down again next to the fire.

John Waukesha smiled at his uncle's persistence, and, walking around the fire, he saw Wakala watching him. The tipi was filled with elders and tribal leaders, and he was going to be the spokesman for this big pow-wow. He was glad that Little Horse, Wakala, and the other two women were inside the lodge for his moment to shine. The two Mounties sat watching him, waiting for his answer. Sergeant Burton was a big man about forty years old with black hair and a deep tan from his years on the Northern Plains. Burton had been a Mountie in Saskatchewan since the Canadian government had sent them there to protect the Indians in 1873. He had been a soldier and was now making a career in the Mounted Police. Corporal Hall was new to Saskatchewan, with no prior experience with Indians. He was a thin, nervous man, and the delay bothered him. He removed his broad brimmed cap and ran his fingers through his curly hair.

"When's he going to speak, Sergeant?" he finally whispered.

"Rest easy, Corporal, the young buck is enjoying the prestige of the moment. He'll answer us soon enough."

Waukesha circled the fire once more and sat down in front of the two white men. He had not seen a white face this close for many moons, since Rusty had left in early spring.

"My father wishes to be friends with the soldiers of the Grandmother," he stated. "He wishes to stay here in peace, so he has told me to tell you the truth. We are Hunkpapa Dakota, called the Sioux by white men, and we are from the Sand Creek River country in the Dakota Territory. Our heart belongs to that country, but our stomachs told us to move elsewhere. We tried to live as peaceful Indians but the white man would not stay out of our lands. He kills our buffalo, our game, and gives whiskey to the young men. Iron Hatchet does not like the firewater for his people and tried to keep it from our tribe, but the white men kept selling it to our young men. They got drunk and acted like fools, falling down and shooting their guns wildly. So, Iron Hatchet moved up into Montana country to avoid the white man. But we found little game to feed our women and children."

Waukesha stood up, and, as he did, caught the eye of Wakala watching him. Her admiring glances pleased him. He continued, raising his arm as he spoke.

"And so we were forced to come further north, seeking only food and peace. We finally found it here by Old Wives Lake where our brothers, the Blackfeet, have welcomed us and fed us. We desire nothing more than to fish this lake, hunt these woods, and live in peace with the government of the Grandmother.

"This is what my uncle has told me to tell the red coat soldiers."

John Waukesha sat down, crossing his legs. His face was stoic as he waited for the Mounties to speak.

Sergeant Burton cleared his throat and spoke. "Tell Iron Hatchet he is welcome as a guest of the Queen, and may stay here as long as his people behave. He may hunt and fish, but he will not steal horses or raid his enemies. He will live in peace with all his brothers, red and white. If your people break the Grandmother's law, you will be sent back to the United States."

The Sergeant finished speaking and waited while young Waukesha translated to Iron Hatchet. He was curious about the young brave's ability to speak English so well. In fact, he didn't even have an accent. Very strange.

The Indians finished talking and Waukesha turned to the white men. "My uncle agrees to live here in peace as it is his fondest wish. But he asks for one favor."

"What is that, Waukesha?"

"He insist that the Queen supply him with coffee in return for him not stealing ponies."

"Agreed," Burton answered, smiling. Iron Hatchet shouted with glee at this news, and grasped the hand of Sergeant Burton, shaking it vigorously.

"Come on, Corporal," Burton said as he stood up. "Let's get back to our post. We'll be back soon enough to see these people and find out more. Waukesha, I will see you again, and tell your uncle I will send the coffee over tomorrow. Good night."

The two Mounties left the lodge and rode their horses out of the dark village toward their post.

John sat down in the center of the Sioux lodge and recounted all of his conversation with the Mounties. It was a proud moment for him. This night had made him a big man in the eyes of his Dakota brothers. The story telling lasted far into the night.

Chapter Eight
WAKALA

Sunrise found John sleeping peacefully in the lodge of Iron Hatchet. The old chief snored loudly in his bed lying next to Calf Woman. Chipeto and Wakala slept close to them, and John and Little Horse were bedded down near the entrance flap. This morning there were three other old braves who had fallen asleep during the long conversation the night before, sleeping in a semi-circle around the fire.

John sat up slowly and rubbed his eyes. The morning air was chilly, and, standing up, he stepped over the slumbering bodies to the fire to warm himself. Wakala was sleeping, only her face showing out of the blanket. Her raven hair was not braided but hung loosely around her face, framing her lovely skin and high cheekbones. She was a beautiful Dakota woman.

As he stared at her, he knew his pounding heart was winning over his logic. He decided he would not fight his feelings any longer; today he would talk to her, and see how she felt about him. If she would marry him, then they would be married. He would worry about the future later, but for now he wanted this beautiful, gentle woman for his wife.

Leaving the lodge, Waukesha walked slowly down the slope toward a stream that ran into the lake and sat down on the wet grass next to a small pool to wait. He knew Wakala would soon be coming down to fetch water for the day. The pine trees blocked this spot from the village, and here John had decided to do his courting. He took the flute out of his shirt and started playing it. It was not a tune, but he moved his fingers across the holes, working up and down a scale, the flute producing a lovely tone for such a primitive instrument. John was engrossed with the flute, blowing softly, enjoying the morning sunshine.

A shadow moved behind him and caught his eye. He turned quickly to see the lovely form of Wakala standing above him, wearing a deer skin dress and high leather moccasins tied up near her knees. She had braided her hair and carried a water basket in her hand. She hesitated briefly before speaking.

"Good morning, John Waukesha. Is that a lover's flute you were playing? Who is it that you court here by the stream? Is some young woman hidden in the bushes or willows?"

John flushed a bright red, his face burning, as this turn of events were not in his plans. He was embarrassed to the point of feeling foolish. Struggling for words, he decided finally to act and overcome his fears. His heart pounding wildly, he walked next to Wakala.

"No, Wakala, there is no one in the bushes except perhaps a rabbit or a mouse." Surprisingly, his voice did not crack. He looked directly into her dark eyes and felt his courage growing.

"The flute was to be played for you. I had intended to play it from the bushes while you gathered water this morning. I had hoped you would not be offended. My heart is full of love for you, and now I have started off very badly."

"Not so badly, John Waukesha," she answered him. "Do not feel embarrassed. I am a widow, you know, and do not need all the normal trappings that go along with courting. Besides the flute should be played only to show what is in one's heart, not for the sake of playing it. The fact that you have finally acted is enough for me."

"I do not understand," John said. "Have you known all along that I would court you?"

"Yes, since the time I first saw you lying wounded in Iron Hatchet's lodge near Squaw's Head. While I helped nurse you, my heart would race every time I touched you. But I speak too boldly."

"No, do not stop. Your words are as sweet as the song of the birds of the air to me; I have felt strongly for you since the first time I saw you."

He pulled her to him and wrapped his arms around her in an embrace, feeling her warm, soft body pressed against his. He had no doubts now.

"Marry me, Wakala," he whispered into her hair.

"Yes, yes, I will. I will be your wife and make you proud of me."

They pulled against each other tightly until Wakala pushed him away.

"Be patient, my love," she said, breathing heavily. "We must do nothing foolish. We can be married right away, and then we shall share the same blanket. Now I must return to camp with my water. Come, walk to the stream with me."

She picked up her basket and walked down the hill. John walked next to her, smiling in disbelief at the conversation that had just taken place. He was going to marry a Dakota girl, and the most beautiful one he had ever seen. *Hoka Hey*! Wait until Little Horse heard the news. Little Horse!

"What about Little Horse?" he blurted out, suddenly worried about his cousin.

"Ahh," she said, "that is the sad part. For he is a fine brave and any woman would be pleased to have him for her husband. But he will soon forget me, and find another wife."

"How shall we tell him, Wakala? It will be a hard thing for me to do."

"Do not worry. We will do the traditional courtship of the blanket this evening. When you and Little Horse come with your blankets I will choose you, and it will be settled.

"I must go now. Please do not think me too bold a woman for speaking to you as I have, but I am a widow and could not go back and pretend to be a young girl again. I did not love Three Fingers, although he was a brave warrior and gentle husband, and I wish to marry a man that I love this time. I will wait anxiously for you to come tonight." She turned away from him, walking up the ridge with her water basket held on her shoulder.

Dakota courting was traditionally done in the evening. John tried to make the day pass quickly, but each hour seemed like a week. He avoided Little Horse all day. He could not face his cousin under the circumstances. He spent the day walking along the lake, sailing rocks over its surface.

At last the sun started to drop below the pines, and he returned to the camp carrying his blanket. As John approached Iron Hatchet's lodge, he was surprised to see Little Horse come around from behind the tipi. His cousin was carrying a blanket.

"Hey, Brother!" he shouted. "I have been waiting for you. I watched you hide in the woods with your blanket and knew you would be showing up here soon, so I brought my own blanket. As I am here first, I will court Wakala first. Good luck, *Hohe*."

John didn't know what to do next. He had seen several suitors stand in line before the tipi of an attractive girl, but he felt embarrassed by this situation. Now he would have to watch while his cousin tried to lure Wakala inside his blanket. He couldn't figure out any other plan of action, so he sat down.

"Good luck to you also, Little Horse. Remember that whoever wins her, we will still be brothers and friends."

As Little Horse stood in front of the lodge, John thought his cousin looked quite handsome. Little Horse had an army blanket wrapped around him with his U.S. Army trooper's hat sitting jauntily on his head. His face was lean and striking, black eyes peering from behind high cheekbones. Today he was wearing large silver earrings and a bear claw necklace. Little Horse began to sing in a deep voice.

"My love, it is your warrior come to see you. Wakala, come out of the lodge, I have been waiting for you."

John didn't think he could ever do that, but Little Horse appeared not the least bit embarrassed by his singing. The young Hunkpapa walked boldly back and forth in front of the lodge, singing louder and louder until the tipi flap opened and Wakala stepped out. Her hair was braided with rabbit fur and she was wearing a cloth dress, brown with gold and green trim. A gold strip was sewn around the waist with fringe hanging down in two separate rows. She looked beautiful and somehow older to John as she stood directly in front of Little Horse, who finished his song.

"Come, my love, I open my blanket to you. Enter that we may be close." Little Horse finished his song and opened his blanket for Wakala to enter.

But she did not move.

"I am honored to have Little Horse come to court me," she said, "but I cannot enter your blanket. My heart belongs to another brave of this tribe."

She turned from him to John, who was still sitting down. He looked up at her for an instant, unable to realize what was expected. Suddenly, he leapt to his feet and opened his blanket.

"Come, Wakala, my heart and my blanket are opened to you. Come to me, my love," he sang.

She walked into his arms without hesitation, and John closed the blanket around her in an embrace. She was really his and his heart soared to the mountaintops as she wrapped her arms around his waist and whispered to him.

"Come, let us speak to Iron Hatchet so we may be married soon. I wish to court no longer."

"Yes," he said, holding her close, "but first I must speak to Little Horse. He is my brother and his heart is sad."

John turned to speak to Little Horse, but he had disappeared into the woods after Wakala chose John.

"Do not worry about Little Horse," Iron Hatchet said, suddenly appearing from behind the tipi. "He is only running away to hide his pain. He is a Dakota man and will soon recover. You watch—he'll be back to congratulate you. But I am here now and I will bless you both. You have my blessings, for I am happy John Waukesha has decided to take a Dakota wife and will stay with us always."

Iron Hatchet smiled broadly at both of them and continued speaking.

"Now let her go. You are not married yet. We will feast tomorrow and you can be married. Calf Woman and Chipeto will build a lodge so you and Wakala will have a place to live. But tonight you cannot sleep in my lodge for it would not be proper, as Wakala will still be sleeping here. Go build yourself a *wickiup* for tonight."

John let go of Wakala reluctantly. "Yes, I will go, but are you sure Little Horse will be okay? He is my brother and I worry for him."

"Go, my son. He will be fine."

John turned and took Wakala by her hand.

"Good night, sweet Wakala. Tomorrow you will be my wife."

"Good night, John Waukesha," she answered. He walked down toward the stream, his heart pounding wildly.

Waukesha built his *wickiup* under a stand of aspens near the spot where he had met Wakala that morning. Humming softly as he worked, the pine branches were soon laced together into a roof for him. He filled the floor with pine needles and started a fire to cook his supper. Darkness settled in and he lay back on the grass, the moonlight reflecting off of the clouds as they sailed overhead. The breeze was warm, and John soon drifted off to sleep next to the fire.

A foot pushed against his ribs, waking him. He opened his eyes to see Little Horse standing above him.

"You sleep too soundly, Waukesha. If I was a Crow or blue coat, you would be dead now."

"You speak the truth, Little Horse, but I feel safe here with the Hunk-papas and the Grandmother's soldiers around. Besides I am probably act-ing a little foolish after today's events. My head is still spinning."

Neither spoke as they stared at the embers of John's fire. Both were feeling a little strange as Wakala was the first problem they had ever had between them. Finally, Little Horse cleared his throat.

"I have come to wish you the blessings of the Great Wakantanka in your marriage with Wakala. I did not act like a man today when I left, but my pride took over. I am glad for you."

Little Horse extended his hand to help pull up John. As he did, John clasped his cousin's hand.

"I am glad you have come back," John told him. "My happiness would not be complete without my brother to share it. Wakala will en-rich my life as a Dakota, but I would not like to be without you as my friend and brother. Very soon I am sure you will find another woman to take as your wife, and then our joy will be total."

"You have spoken as my heart feels," Little Horse said. "We knew one of us would lose and I am man enough to bear it. Our love and friendship will not end over such a little matter as a woman. Go back to sleep now. We will have the wedding feast tomorrow, when the sun is high in the sky. You must be well-rested so Wakala will not be disap-pointed with her new husband on her wedding night."

They laughed at Little Horse's joke, and stood silently for a minute.

"I will go now," Little Horse announced.

"We shall celebrate tomorrow at my wedding feast, and I will be honored to have you there. And when Wakala bears her first son, it shall be named for you."

"Thank you, Brother," Little Horse called as he disappeared into the darkness.

Iron Hatchet was down by the lake early on the next day. He se-lected the site for the honeymoon lodge: a small clearing that opened up to the lakeshore. It was surrounded by pine-covered hills with a small stream flowing next to the clearing. The main village was well on the far side of the east ridge, so John and Wakala would have their privacy. After two weeks or so they would move back with the rest of the Hunkpapas and start leading a normal tribal life. After Little Horse and Iron Hatchet dragged the lodge poles to the site, their part was done, and Chipeto and Calf-Woman began setting up the tipi. It was constructed in slightly over two hours. The women started a fire and began cooking the antelope meat and wild turnips. Although it was called a wedding feast, it would really only be a simple meal, ending quickly so the honeymoon could begin.

When the preparation was nearly finished, Little Horse went to find his cousin. John was sitting near his *wickiup*, staring at the dying fire.

"*Hoka Hey*, Brother," Little Horse called out as he approached. "Why do you look so pale?"

"Oh, my brother, I am feeling very nervous. My stomach is as hard as a tree trunk. Perhaps I cannot go through with this."

"Aww, I believe you are scared. Don't tell me a little woman like Wakala strikes fear into the heart of the Ree slayer."

"Yes, I'm afraid that's so."

"Do not fear, Waukesha, I will help you. We will make you look as handsome as the finest war pony. Wakala will be speechless with your beauty."

Little Horse sat John in front of him, and, sticking his fingers in a small bowl, painted two yellow stripes down his cousin's cheeks, stopping at his neck. He placed his own elk tooth's necklace on John, laying it over the blue army coat he wore. Rubbing grease in Waukesha's hair, he tied rabbit fur to the braids and stuck an eagle feather in each braid.

"*Ho Ho!*" Little Horse exclaimed. "You would please any Dakota woman today. Come, let's go to the honeymoon lodge before Wakala arrives."

They entered the lodge to find Iron Hatchet already there, wearing the full head bonnet John had seen on the mountaintop near the Greasy Grass River. Manter sat next to the chief, along with the two old men from the tribal council. All were adorned in their finest clothes with fancy beadwork and feathers, and they were laughing as John and Little Horse entered.

"Come sit here next to me," Iron Hatchet called out. "Your bride will be here soon and the meal will begin."

"I am glad to see my friend Manter here. He does me honor by coming," John said as he sat down, crossing his legs.

Manter only nodded and patted John's shoulder, who indulged himself with the pleasant odor of Calf Woman's cooking, which bubbled away in the iron kettle over the fire. The whole scene was slightly unreal to John. He couldn't believe that this was his wedding day. Chipeto and Calf Woman soon entered the darkened tipi and sat down behind the men. The two women smiled broadly at John when they passed him.

Leaning behind Iron Hatchet, John whispered to Little Horse. "Where is she? Perhaps she is not coming and has left the camp."

"Rest easy," Little Horse answered him. "She will be here soon. Watch the door, I think I can hear her coming."

The entrance was darkened for an instant as the trim figure of Wakala entered the lodge and stood before the fire, looking at her lover. She wore a buckskin dress: the long fringe hanging from the sleeves and skirt to the high beaded moccasins she was wearing. Braided with rabbit fur, her long hair hung down over her shoulders, almost covering a yellow bead necklace. John thought she had never looked more beautiful.

Iron Hatchet stood up and, taking Wakala by her arm, sat her down next to John. He stood above them and spoke.

"The wedding ceremony of the Sioux is very simple, John Waukesha. A man takes a woman and that is all there is to it. But I will say a few words, as is the custom of the white man.

"The Great Spirit brought John Waukesha back from the dead to his people, and now he has chosen Waukesha to take Wakala as his wife. Perhaps he was sent to replace Three Fingers, who was killed two moons ago. Now, these two will be joined as man and wife, and Wakantanka will surely smile on this wedding. They will grow old together and produce many Dakota children. May they and their children always know the peace and joy we know this day in the land of the Grandmother. Take her hand, John Waukesha, and protect her always, for she is a Dakota woman and will make you a fine wife.

"Now, Calf Woman and Chipeto serve the wedding couple first and we shall enjoy the wedding meal."

"Thank you, Father. Your words were spoken like a true Dakota chief but I have something to say to you before we eat. Although you have said that I was not to give you ponies for my wife, I felt I must give you some gift.

"Little Horse, bring me the present for Iron Hatchet."

The young brave sprung to his feet and, bending over, left the lodge. In a minute, he returned, carrying a large basket, which he gave to John. Opening the basket, John took out a brand new coffee pot. He proudly handed it to Iron Hatchet.

"Here," he said. "Sergeant Burton was able to get this for me with some American dollars I still had. Now your coffee will taste as good as Rusty White Hair's does."

"*Ho Ho!*" Iron Hatchet exclaimed. "You have made me a fine present. Here Calf Woman, use this shining new pot now and we shall have some fine coffee to go with the wedding meal."

The meal moved along quickly, the men telling stories and laughing while the women talked quietly. The sun was dipping low in the sky when Iron Hatchet stood up and announced it was time to leave. John felt a tinge of fear as he watched them departing up the hill toward the village. He was nervous and not sure how he would be with a woman. Standing outside, he waited too long as he watched the visitors disappear. Swallowing hard, he reentered the darkened tipi.

His eyes adjusted slowly until he could see Wakala lying in the bed, a blanket pulled around her neck. Her hair was loose, lying softly on her shoulders. Nervously, he walked over to her and knelt down, looking at her.

"Get in, John Waukesha," she finally said. "It is time."

He took off his shirt and climbed under the blanket, leaving his pants on. His heart pounded wildly as he slid in next to her and put his arms around her. She was naked and pushed against him.

"Oh, Wakala," he murmured and pressed his body against her.

Chapter Nine

THE GRIZZLY

Above Sergeant Burton's desk was a large, stuffed white owl, standing on a bar mounted between a pair of elk's antlers. The owl had been with Burton for many years, and, when the Sergeant was feeling good, he liked to sit back with his hands behind his head and study the owl while he did his thinking. Right now, he felt fine. He had just completed the September 1876 report to Headquarters, and it had been a very good report. The territory under his jurisdiction had been calm for several months; even the influx of Iron Hatchet's Hunkpapas had not caused serious problems. The Hunkpapas were behaving themselves and things were peaceful in the province.

Sergeant Burton's thoughts were interrupted by the sound of a horse approaching. He walked outside the cabin and sat down on the porch. His number two man, Corporal Hall, rode up the path and dismounted. He wrapped the horse's reins around the wood railing.

"Everything okay on your rounds, Thomas?" Burton asked.

"Fine, Sergeant," Corporal Hall answered. "Nothing of particular interest to report. I rode beyond the lake to see the settlers out there, but they haven't had any problems with the new Indians. All in all, it's going pretty smoothly.

"Old man Sutton did mention that a grizzly bear had killed one of his calves last week. Maybe, if we get some time, we can head out that way to kill it, and one of us could have a new coat for this winter."

"Did the old man actually see the bear?" Burton asked, as Hall sat down next to his friend on the cabin's porch.

"Better than that. He shot at it as it ran into the woods, but Sutton's sure he didn't hit the bear."

"Damn," Burton interrupted, "I sure hope he didn't hit it. Nothing more dangerous than a wounded grizzly.

"Tell you what, Corporal, while you take my reports into the settlement for posting this afternoon, I'm going to ride out that way, and try to pick up the grizzly's tracks to make sure he's not bleeding. Then, maybe in a day or two, the two of us will go after him."

"That sounds like a good idea."

"C'mon, I worked up a real hunger making my rounds this morning and I want some lunch. Do we have any fresh meat? It seems to me the game is getting scarcer all the time around here."

Because of this scarcity, John Waukesha was forced to go further and further from the village to find meat. The lack of game forced the Dakotas and Blackfeet ever closer to the white man's farms, creating a potential danger to all concerned. Still, John stayed in the woods, never going near the whites, where there could be trouble. Life in Canada had been good to him.

On this cool early October day—the Moon when the Leaves Turn Yellow—the young Hunkpapa half-breed was hunting in a ravine far from camp, near the western shore of Old Wives Lake. Above him, the autumn sun shone brilliantly through the trees, warming him as he lay under a white pine, waiting for game to come to the stream below.

He had buried himself in brown pine needles, and, although he was invisible in the forest shadows, no animals had strayed into his bow's range.

Lying motionless, his body began to cramp. Finally, the aching in his legs became unbearable and he sat up, shaking off the pine needles. He bent his knees up to his chest and pulled hard, trying to limber up his stiff muscles.

"Ohh," he groaned as he stretched. "It has been another bad day. Wakantanka still does not smile on me."

The sun was still fairly high in the sky, so he decided to try a different location before returning to camp empty-handed. He walked up the side of the ravine to a hilltop that was treeless except for one large ponderosa pine. The magnificent tree stood over one hundred and fifty feet high and John Waukesha stopped to rest alongside it. The valley lay below him, the pine forest broken up by an occasional settler's farm. A single cow could be seen grazing lazily in a pasture. A bald eagle slowly circled over the fields, gliding gracefully on the winds over the brown farmland. John watched quietly as the eagle winged its way up the valley and sailed over his head toward the mountains.

The Dakota's attention moved quickly to the underbrush at the clearing's edge, which cracked with the noise of breaking branches. Waukesha slid an arrow on his bow and knelt down next to the pine, hoping it was a moose or wapiti, the elk. His tribe could sure use a large kill for food. The brown undergrowth shook as the beast pushed through it. A giant grizzly bear stepped into the clearing. The bear stood on his hind legs, well over eight feet tall, as he looked around, sniffing the air and growling.

"*Hoka Hey!*" John muttered. "He is the biggest bear I have ever seen. I would hate to have those great yellow teeth bite me. This must be Mato, the sacred bear who walks like a man. Perhaps he will not see me and pass on into the forest. One swipe of those huge paws, and I would be sent to the Spirit World."

John continued studying the great animal until he saw something unusual. Next to a white spot of fur on the chest of the bear was blood, dried and matted as if it were several days old. Mato could barely lift one foreleg because of this wound.

"That's why you are so angry, Mato," John whispered. He felt a tinge of fear as he realized the danger of his situation. His bow and arrow seemed very inadequate for such a large bear. He prayed the grizzly would turn and reenter the trees, but Mato did not go back into the woods. He had caught a scent in the air that was familiar, which caused his anger to rise. The smell was man.

Mato dropped to all fours and moved up the ridge toward the ponderosa to find the source of the man smell. Like all bears, Mato had poor eyesight and couldn't yet see the young Indian buck, but the man scent was growing stronger the closer he got to the ancient tree. He circled the tree searching for his enemy.

As Waukesha moved around the tree, keeping it between him and the bear, he raised his bow. Mato was going to charge, and perhaps some arrow wounds would slow the bear down long enough for him to escape. John stepped from the tree and pulled his bowstring tight.

"Mato!" he shouted. The grizzly stood up, towering over the Dakota, ready to charge. *Zing*—the arrow flew, striking the bear in the chest, where it buried deep. Mato roared in anger, and, dropping to all fours, he charged as John fired another arrow, hitting the bear in his left shoulder.

John turned and ran, loading his bow while Mato quickly closed the distance between them. He knew the grizzly was close and he stopped, firing another arrow. He aimed for the bear's open jaws, but Mato was struck in the forehead and the arrow bounced harmlessly away. Standing his ground, John drew his steel knife and began chanting an old Sioux death song, knowing he would not live through this fight.

The grizzly, somewhat confused by John's stand, stood up on his hind legs, momentarily halting his charge. Bleeding freely from his wounds, Mato sprang forward and crushed Waukesha inside his paws. John felt the massive strength of the bear pull him forward into the bear's belly; he could smell Mato's hot breath. As he was slammed into the mass of fur, John pushed his knife into Mato's belly, cutting a foot long slash of red into the brown fur.

Howling in rage, the grizzly stepped back and smashed his opponent across the head, knocking the young man head over heels through the air. Struggling to his feet, Waukesha held his knife up as Mato roared into him again. John leapt into the charging bear, driving his knife into the grizzly's shoulder. Mato clamped his jaws down on the young brave's arm. While the bear's claws ripped open his back, John screamed in pain as the yellow teeth tore the muscles and bones. John drove the knife again and again into Mato's neck. Blood covered both of them, and John gasped for breath against the bear's furry chest. He had mortally wounded the grizzly, but he knew the bear would kill him before he died. Waukesha's arm was badly chewed, his back torn open, and the bear was crushing the air from his lungs. Wakala's lovely face passed before him in a dream while he chanted a Dakota death song. His mind became confused as he tried to fight the bear, his strength bleeding from him. Soon he would pass out, and the pain would stop.

The bear staggered backwards, dragging John with him as he fell. Mato released his grip on his prisoner, and John felt the searing pain in his arm ease. Mato was dead. Rolling his head from the grizzly's chest John could barely see a man's form standing above him. The man wore black boots, a red coat, and a wide-brimmed hat. His face was not clear at first but, finally, John was able to recognize him.

"Sergeant Burton," he mumbled softly as blackness filled his mind. He lay his head down gently on the bear's chest and passed out.

Burton had spent most of the afternoon looking for the grizzly after Mr. Sutton had shown him where he had last seen the giant bear the previous week. Although he swore he had missed the grizzly, Burton wanted to make sure. A wounded grizzly was just about the meanest animal alive, and the Mountie didn't want a danger like that roaming his territory. The trail Sutton put him on was cold, so he set out through the hills looking for a fresh one, and soon found it. Following this trail, he found the bear had slept in a small hollow in the base of a large hemlock tree. The needles were still compacted with plenty of bear fur for evidence. Examining it closely, Burton saw the dark matted needles and knew the substance to be blood. Sutton had wounded the grizzly. There was enough dried blood to show that it was a serious wound, making this bear a killer and any man he found would be a likely victim.

Sergeant Burton surmounted the hill above where John Waukesha and Mato were fighting without even knowing they were there. Staring in disbelief, he watched the incredible struggle take place within fifty yards of him. How he had not heard the thrashing and growling, he did not know. A dust cloud surrounded the Indian and bear as the Mountie dismounted and cautiously approached them.

"Waukesha," he exclaimed as he recognized the Indian for the first time. The brave was slashing at the bear's neck and shoulder as the grizzly chewed on Waukesha's left arm.

My God, Burton thought, *they've killed each other.* The Sioux was covered with blood while the bear's intestines hung down where it stood. The giant of the forest finally stood up straight and fell backward, dead upon landing.

Burton ran up to them and stood over the two bodies. The young Indian was lying on top of the dead bear. "Oh, Waukesha, I am so sorry I was too late," he said. "But what a fight you put up. You actually killed this beast armed only with a knife before he killed you."

He bent down to lift the young Indian off of the bear. Waukesha slowly lifted his head and said, "Sergeant Burton."

"My God, you're alive," he shouted.

He dressed the young man's arm wound as best he could, wrapping it with the bandages from the first aid kit in his saddle bags, and gave him water from his canteen. Then, leading his horse closer, he slid his Indian friend over the saddle. The trip would be rough on a badly wounded man, but he could do no more for him until they got back to his post. There, they could give him proper treatment from the doctor in the settlement. Looking once more at the huge grizzly lying harmlessly on the hillside, Burton led his horse slowly down the hill. Waukesha's limbs dangled freely as they slowly descended to the flat surface of the valley below.

Sergeant Burton sent Corporal Hall to Iron Hatchet immediately upon his return with the news that Waukesha had been seriously wounded and was being treated by the white doctor. Wakala insisted that she be allowed to help care for her husband. Burton readily agreed to this, as he was too busy to give John the daily nursing he would require. Wakala moved into the Mounties' log cabin, sleeping on a blanket on the floor next to Waukesha's bed. She dressed his wounds, fed him what hot liquids he would take, and prayed to Wankantanka to let her husband live.

John's wounds, other than his arm, were not as severe as Burton had feared. His back and side were badly lacerated but no serious muscle damage had been done. The triceps muscle in his left arm had been badly chewed by the grizzly's teeth but the bone was intact and time would heal this wound. The loss of blood was his most serious problem. Wakala watched him through five days of deep and fitful sleep as the infection passed through his body. He would jump wildly, calling out her name or that of Little Horse, while his body burnt with fever. Wakala could only hold his hand and pray. The white doctor could do no more for him; his life was in the hands of the Great Spirit.

On the sixth day, the fever broke and Wakala thanked Wakantanka for the life of her husband. As she wiped his face she spoke to him.

"John Waukesha, John Waukesha, can you hear me? It is Wakala. Wake up my husband. Wake up."

John slowly opened his eyes, the bright mid-day light causing him to blink repeatedly. He focused his eyes, finally making out the familiar face of his wife bending over him.

"Ahh, Wakala," he said softly, "Mato did not kill me after all. I thought I would never see you again in this world."

"No, my husband, it is Mato who is dead. His fur is in the village being made into a coat for you by Chipeto, and Calf Woman makes his teeth and claws into a necklace for Waukesha, the great bear killer."

He smiled at her and took her hand in his as she started crying gently now.

"Have you been with me long?" he asked. "I don't know what happened after that giant animal crushed me into his chest. Where are we?"

"This is the lodge of the red coat, Sergeant Burton. He found you in the death grip of the bear and brought you here so the white doctor could care for you. I have helped as much as I could while you slept for five days now. At first, we thought you had lost too much blood to survive, but you are a true warrior and would not die. My heart has been so heavy with fear."

She began to cry harder now, the tears rushing out in torrents as she laid her head on his chest. He placed his hand on her hair and gently stroked her long braids. They would be closer than ever from this time on.

The weeks passed quickly for John and Wakala as he recovered rapidly, growing stronger everyday. The two Mounties welcomed the change in their daily routine. Wakala prepared all their meals and the food took a decided step toward improvement. The evening meal, usually served around eight o'clock, took on special meaning for all four of them, for the conversation was lively and interesting. Sergeant Burton insisted that Wakala sit down and eat with them, and she tried to join in whenever she could. Her knowledge of English rapidly increased and she followed the stories being told. The cabin was warm from the glow of the fireplace and the four were becoming friends. John had a natural liking for Burton from the first meeting and his timely rescue from the grizzly had sealed this bond even tighter.

Still, he had been reluctant to answer the Mounties when they asked him for the truth about his past. After all, Burton wanted to know how did a Sioux Indian end up being called John? Starting slow-

ly at first, John had found telling the story much easier than he antici-
pated. The years in Chicago and the more recent times in Dakota flew
by as he talked for several hours, only altering the tribe's involvement
at Little Big Horn. It felt good to share his experiences with a white
man who understood nature and the freedom of the West, and was in
full sympathy with the Indians.

They sat silently for a moment when Waukesha finished. Finally Burton spoke: "You have led a fantastic life for being just a young
man, John, and you are obviously happy living as a Dakota. Will you
stay with them?"

"I think so, Sergeant, although I must return soon to see my
mother. She will be so pleased with Wakala. I would like to bring my
mother back to live among the Dakotas if she wants to return."

Looking somber, Sergeant Burton spoke again. "I don't think
that would be wise, for though your Sioux brethren may visit here, the
Canadian government does not recognize Iron Hatchet's band as Canadian Indians. I don't think they will ever grant them a permanent
reservation. In other words, your tribe may someday have to return to
the States, where things will not be so pleasant.

"You know for a fact that the game around here is becoming
very scarce. It would be hard on a white woman to live on an American reservation."

"That's right," Corporal Hall jumped in. "Leave her back in the
comfort of Chicago."

"You both speak the truth," John told them. "Besides it was only
a passing thought on my part. My mother's health has not been too
good the last few years, and she is happy in Chicago with her friends
and memories.

"Tell me, Sergeant, do you think the Grandmother will force us
to leave Old Wives Lake? We have been very happy here."

"The Canadian government will not force you to leave, but it will
not give you your own land, and you know this place cannot support
both you and the Blackfeet for too much longer. We will supply ra-

tions, but times will be hard for your people. It is sad to say but some-day Iron Hatchet will have to return to the Dakota Territory. I am try-ing to fight for him, but I am just one man."

"Yes," John said, "you are only one man, but a fine one. If all whites were like you, we could return to our home in Dakota with no fear in our hearts."

"Thank you, Waukesha."

"I only speak what is in my heart. Perhaps we will not have to leave the land of the Grandmother. Perhaps her heart will change and we may have our own land."

"I hope you're right, my friend," Burton told him. "But even if the Hunkpapa must return, you could stay here and settle. You are half-white and could reside on these lands and farm. That way at least you and Wakala and your children would be free."

"No, I could not leave my brothers to suffer on a reservation. They will need my help, as I know the white man, and would be able to speak for them. I am a Dakota, if my people must live on reserva-tions, then I will live on a reservation. I will work to free us so we may fly like the wind over the prairies again. I cannot believe Wakantanka has deserted his people forever."

"That decision is up to you," the Mountie agreed. "It is some-thing for you to think about.

"But now, let's have some more coffee and talk of more pleas-ant things. It looks like our first real snow is coming tonight and the corporal and I will be in for a rough day tomorrow, so let's en-joy this evening."

John sat at the sergeant's desk the next day, studying a map of Saskatchewan, which was part of the Canadian Northwest Territory, in an effort to learn the entire area, so he could expand his hunting range when he returned to the village. It would soon be time to return to the Hunkpapa village and the cold of his tipi, even though he had enjoyed the warmth of the cabin, the tables and chairs, and the softness of a real bed. He would feel certain reluctance upon leaving this warm cabin, but he still yearned for the freedom of his own lodge.

He looked up from the desk as the door opened and Wakala entered.

"*Hoa*, Little Horse approaches," she said.

They both walked outside onto the porch. John called out to his cousin. "Come inside, Little Horse. Wakala will make us some fresh coffee that will surely warm you up."

Little Horse wore his buffalo robe and long pants for warmth, and, sliding off Swift Moon's back, he walked through the half foot of snow onto the porch.

"Come in," Waukesha said, putting his arm around Little Horse's shoulder. "The red coats are gone and we are alone."

"It is good to see you looking so well, Waukesha. We have missed you and Wakala at Iron Hatchet's lodge."

The three entered the cabin and sat down around the table while the young woman made hot coffee.

"It is very warm in here," Little Horse said sliding his robe down on the chair. Over his buckskin shirt hung a bear's claw necklace made from gigantic claws. He straightened them out as Waukesha looked in puzzlement.

"That is a fine necklace you wear, Little Horse. Is it new?"

"Yes," Little Horse answered, smiling. "It is really nothing. I found it near a huge ponderosa pine awhile back."

"Tell me, Brother, were those claws still in a grizzly bear's paws at that time?"

"Why, yes they were. But the bear was dead, probably from old age, as he was very skinny and run-down looking. I figured the claws were mine as there was no one around to claim them.

"Does my brother know something more about how this bear may have died?" Little Horse could hardly contain his laughter now as his joke was going very well. Wakala giggled as she watched the two cousins banter back and forth.

"I do know a little more, Cousin," John told him as he stood up and walked around behind Little Horse. "Because that bear put up a terrific fight with a brave Dakota before he died. They fought like this."

John jumped on his cousin and they tumbled onto the floor, wrestling and flipping each other over. Little Horse was laughing so hard he was near tears. John rolled his opponent on his back and sat on his chest, his knees pinning Little Horse down.

"Now give me my necklace, for I know those large claws only too well. They belonged to Mato and now they are mine."

"Yes, yes. They are yours," Little Horse gasped. "Take them and wear them proudly. My little joke is finished."

John slipped the bear claw necklace around his neck and stood proudly above his cousin. The necklace was heavy, but he would bear the weight gladly. He was the slayer of Mato.

Little Horse stayed with them through the afternoon, telling stories and drinking the Mounties' coffee. It was a pleasant day for the three of them, and, as the sun settled behind the forest, the young brave rode off at sundown. It had been a good day with good friends.

The young couple stood on the porch for a long time, watching the Dakota buck disappear into the shadows of the forest. It was snowing faster now; the wind and snow fell on their faces as they enjoyed the chill of the air, hands clutched together.

Soon, another rider could be seen coming through the snow. Waukesha could make out the form of his friend Sergeant Burton as the horse moved slowly against the blowing wind toward the cabin. Burton waved as he dismounted, and, entering the cabin, he brushed the snow from his clothes. After taking a cup of hot coffee from Wakala, he stood near the fire warming his backside.

"Feels like some real winter is about to blow in," he said. "I left my gloves here at the cabin and my hands just about froze off. Next time I ride to town, I'll remember to take them with me for sure."

"I think you are right," Waukesha answered, standing by the Mountie near the fire. "The north wind is bringing much snow with it this time."

"It sure feels like it, Waukesha. By the way, I have a letter for you." Burton reached inside his uniform and pulled out the letter. "It was at the post office at Fort Saskatchewan today. It's been sent all over western Canada before it reached here. Not too many people know you as John Holcumb."

John read the envelope and knew it was from his mother. His heart pounded quickly as he ripped it open and read the letter.

"What does it say?" Wakala asked. "Is it from your mother?"

"It is. She is very ill and thinks she is going to die. She said that she would have written me earlier but did not know how to get in touch with me. Apparently the Chicago newspapers have printed stories about the Sioux fleeing to Canada, so she sent the letter up here.

"It's really something that this letter ever found me."

"What's the date on the letter, John?" Burton asked.

"It's August 12th, two months old. Perhaps my mother is already dead without my seeing her. I should have returned earlier."

"Do not talk like that," Wakala said. "I am sure your mother is better by now. The Great Spirit takes care of mothers."

"Thank you, Wakala, but I am worried about her. She would not write me if she were not dying. She really wanted me to stay with the Dakotas. Her doctor is an old friend and he would not lie to her. I must go to her."

"I will go with you," Wakala said.

"No, I am afraid that is not possible. Winter will soon be hard upon us. The trip will take many weeks and be very hard. It is too dangerous for you. Besides I will have to travel as a white man when I re-enter the United States or I might get shot. No, it is better you stay with Iron Hatchet, and I will return just as soon as I can." John squeezed her to him. She did not argue with him, and, taking Waukesha's hand, she held it firmly to reassure him of her understanding.

John stared at the letter a minute and looked at his friend. "Sergeant Burton, will you look after my wife while I am gone. She will stay with Iron Hatchet, but could you keep an eye on her?"

"I would consider it an honor, for you two are very dear to me. Don't worry, she will be well cared for."

"Thank you," Waukesha said, clasping Burton's hand.

"We will move her out to the Hunkpapa village in the morning, and I will set out on my journey. Iron Hatchet and Little Horse will welcome her company, and Chipeto and Calf Woman will be glad to have their sister back."

"I'm sure they will," Burton answered. "C'mon John, let's look at the map and we can plan the route for your trip to Chicago."

Chapter Ten
CHICAGO

Chicago hadn't changed much in the two years since John had left for the Dakotas. It seemed more crowded than ever, and the people were just as unfriendly. As he left the train, the pushing and shoving crowd closed in on him, and he could feel the mass of humanity crushing him.

This is worse than being caught in a buffalo herd, he thought. He had his hair tucked up under a hat, and had borrowed some clothes from Sergeant Burton, so he didn't look much like a Dakota brave. A large woman stepped hard on his moccasins and John grimaced in pain, rubbing his foot as he was bumped around. He finally stopped trying to avoid the other combatants, and, plunging ahead, the crowd carried him outside of the station and into the crisp November morning.

John walked to the shore of Lake Michigan and headed toward his mother's house. He prayed silently to the Great Spirit to keep his mother alive until he was able to see her. Breaking into a jog, the still blue waters of Lake Michigan seemed a strange contrast to the dirty city of Chicago with its foul smelling air. He missed the sweet cold air of his people's home in the Dakotas or Canada.

Turning away from the lake, he started up Hill Street on the new wooden sidewalks, built since he left. The hard sidewalk felt strange to his feet, which were used to the soft grass of the prairies. He saw his mother's flat, two-story house and began to run. The house seemed older than ever as he entered the hallway and ran up the stairs to his mother's door. It was locked.

Knocking, he called out quietly. "Mother, Mother, are you home? It's your son, John. Do you hear me?"

He could hear movement within and smiled, knowing she was alive. The door opened, but it was not his mother who stood in front of him.

"Rusty!" he exclaimed, hugging his old friend.

The huge trapper lifted John off the floor and swung him into the room. "Well, you young pup," Rusty laughed, "where in the hell have you been? Your mother wrote you months ago. I figured you never got the letter, or, even worse, I thought maybe you was killed by the cavalry or somethin'."

"No, I've been alright, Rusty. The letter never found me till October up in Canada, and I started back right away.

"How's my mother?"

Rusty's eyebrows furrowed deeply.

"She ain't good, Johnny Boy. The old saw-bones say's she ain't going to hang on too much longer. I believe she would've gone ahead and died months ago, except she kept saying she was going to wait for her Johnny to come home first."

John listened to his friend's hard words. So his mother was as seriously ill as she had indicated in her letter.

"Well thank you for the truth, Rusty. I want to hear all about how you got here and what's happened to you, but first I want to see my mother. Is she awake?"

"Yeah, she's awake all right. That's one feisty lady you got for a mother. She's lying up in her bed in there makin' you some fancy moccasins. I swear she made me hunt all over Chicago for deerskin, so's her little Johnny could have some pretty new shoes. The doctor told her to just lie still and save her strength, but she keeps on working. C'mon, I'll take you in."

The large man walked over to the bedroom door and knocked gently. "Mrs. Holcumb, I got a visitor here to see you. Are you proper?

The voice came softly through the door. "A visitor? Who in the world is it, Rusty? Bring her in so I can see who it is."

Rusty opened the door slightly and stuck his huge head inside. "It ain't no her I got here, but some young Injun just back from the Wild West."

Pushing the door open, John stepped into the room and saw his mother propped up in her iron bed, covered with an afghan quilt. Her hair was totally gray, she was very thin, and she looked tired. But, at the sight of her son, those eyes sparkled the bright blue of her youth.

"Johnny!" she called out, opening her arms to him. He knelt next to the bed and embraced her. Rusty closed the door and left them alone, knowing that sometimes folks ought to be alone.

John hugged his mother tightly, feeling how thin she had become. "How are you, Mother? I was worried all the way back. How do you feel?"

"Oh, I'm all right now. I've been awful worried about you, but you're back safely, so I'm going to be just fine.

"My, you look so handsome and so grown up. You're no longer the boy I kissed goodbye at the railroad station. I was so proud to read your letters about the buffalo hunt, and I know your father is still smiling over that adventure."

"Yes, it was a great moment for me. I have never been happier at any time in my life."

"Rusty has told me how very happy you were. He is a good man, and he told me many things that you didn't mention in your letters. He's been so kind."

"How did he end up here, Mother? I sure was surprised to see him here when I opened the front door."

"Well, he came to see me in August to see whether or not you had written to him through me. Apparently you and him have some sort of understanding about that. Of course, you hadn't written for some time and never mentioned a meeting with Rusty in any of your letters. About that time I was feeling very, very sickly."

She stopped momentarily and took a drink of water. All the excitement was tiring her, and, closing her eyes, she laid there, quietly holding John's hand. Her hand felt extremely warm. Opening her eyes, she continued slowly, her voice cracking slightly.

"As I said, I was very sick, and Rusty immediately took over nursing me. The doctor couldn't stay all the time and I couldn't afford a nurse, so he insisted on helping. As I really didn't have much choice in the matter, he just stayed and he's really been a godsend. I can't even go to the market anymore, and I probably would have starved to death by now if it weren't for him."

"He is the best," John said. "He helped me a great deal on the trip out West."

"He thinks very highly of you too, John. He has missed you near as much as I have."

She stopped talking and laid her head back on the pillow. He watched her silently, and soon he realized she was asleep. He pulled the afghan around her shoulders and kissed her gently on the forehead. Closing the curtains, he quietly walked out of the room.

Rusty sat deeply on the large green sofa, his feet propped on the frail oval shaped table. His hair looked longer and whiter than ever.

"How is she?" he asked, as John sat down next to him.

"She's sleeping now. She seems to tire so easily. Is it always like that?"

"Yep, her strength fades awful fast. But I saw the look on her face when she saw you and that made her as happy as I've seen her. She'll sleep well tonight."

"What does the doctor say about her?"

"Frankly, he thought she'd be dead by now, cause somethin' is eating up her insides, and he can't do nothin' about it. He gives her medicine for the pain, but he can't stop the dying going on inside her. She knows it too, but you couldn't tell from talkin' to her. She's the bravest damn person I ever know'd."

John heard the word he knew was coming, but it still shocked him: dying.

"We'll do what we can for her," John said. "I don't know how to thank you for taking care of my mother, a total stranger to you. Thank you, Rusty."

John and Rusty served her beef soup that evening and it seemed to strengthen her. Rusty joined them at the insistence of John's mother, sitting in a large over-stuffed chair next to the bed. John cleared away the china and returned to his mother's bedside.

"Sit down, John," his mother said, "and tell us of your recent adventures. The last we heard you were going to Canada with Iron Hatchet's band, and we assumed you were still there. When did you finally receive my letter?"

"It was in October, while I was living with a Canadian Mountie named Sergeant Burton. He was the one that found your letter and brought it to me."

"Why were you living with the Mounties?" Rusty interrupted.

"Well, the truth of the matter is, I had been in a fight with a wounded grizzly, and he tore me up pretty good. I've got his claws with me in my bag."

"Oh, John," his mother broke in, "a grizzly. My Lord, it's lucky you're alive. The Mountie must have taken real good care of you."

"He did, but he had some help. My wife, Wakala, did most of the nursing." John did not explain further, letting the impact of his words set in. He was enjoying Rusty and Mother's befuddlement, knowing that they had never heard of Wakala.

Rusty's curiosity finally prevailed. "Listen, boy, and excuse me, ma'am, who in the hell is this Wakala? Seems I don't recall hearing nothin' about her before."

"Yes," Mrs. Holcumb chimed in, "are you really married?"

Smiling, John answered. "It's true, Mother. Wakala was widowed at the battle of Little Big Horn, when Iron Hatchet took her in. I loved her from the start and we were married in the Moon of the Fallen Leaves. She is not only beautiful and intelligent, but a good Sioux wife and we have been very happy."

They embraced and Rusty patted him on his back in celebration. "You old son of a rattler. You sure are full of surprises."

"Rusty, get out the old bottle of sherry. We should toast the new bridegroom and his bride, even though she is far away," Mrs. Holcumb said.

They drank the sherry and talked on through the evening, one that John would cherish for many years.

His mother's memory was still very good, and she was very curious about the old tribal members. She was delighted to learn about the good health of her brother-in-law, Iron Hatchet, and her nephew, Little Horse. She hadn't known Chipeto, but had fond remembrances of Calf Woman, who had been very kind to her when she lived with the Dakotas.

The hour had grown late when Rusty excused himself to turn in.

"Good night, Rusty," they called after him, as he closed the bedroom door behind him. They were silent briefly.

"Oh, Johnny," she said with a contented sigh, "it is so good to see you again. I was afraid I would die before seeing you. I thank God for that."

"Mother, don't talk like that. You're not going to die. I'm home with you and you're going to be fine."

"No," she insisted, "no use denying the truth. I am dying, and, now that I know you are okay, I'm going to join your father. I've missed him all these years and it's my time to go. My life has been incomplete since that handsome brave was taken from me, and I don't want to wait any longer."

John, at a loss for words, sat silently next to her. Although he had hardened on the plains, he felt like a little boy again. There was nothing he could say; his mother's mind was made up.

She pulled herself up on her pillows and smiled at him. "Don't worry, we'll all be together again in a better world, where whites and Indians will live in peace. When I'm gone, I want you to sell this house and go back to the Dakotas and to your wife. There is no life for you in Chicago. You and Rusty would suffocate and die here. You'll have money to buy some land if you want. You can live as a free man and teach your children the ways of the Dakotas."

"I am going back," he answered, "but I will live with Iron Hatchet's tribe, so my children will be raised like true Dakotas."

"Perhaps so," she said, "but I fear all the Indians will soon be put on reservations because of the Custer Massacre. From the newspaper stories, I gather the Army plans to eliminate all free Indians. The reservation life would be hard on you, and your staying would not help the others. You think about my words carefully, Johnny."

"I will, but for now I will stay with Iron Hatchet's Hunkpapas."

"You are a good son," she said, squeezing his hand. "I'm tired now, we'll talk more in the morning."

"Good night," he said, bending down to kiss her forehead. "Sleep well." She was asleep by the time he blew out the lamp and closed her door quietly.

Although her health deteriorated rapidly over the next month, she still enjoyed conversing with John and Rusty about the prairie life. She was constantly tired and steadily lost weight, barely able to eat more than broth. They cared for her as best they could, talking of the Christmas about to come. Decorations were hung in her room, but she had told them that she would not be there for Christmas. They found her dead on the morning of December twenty-third.

It was mid-winter when the funeral took place, but John and Rusty were unable to return to Canada. January, February, and March dragged by, and it was not until April that they were able to sell the house. John received five hundred dollars for the house, plus two thousand more from his mother's bank savings and life insurance policy. He left the house feeling some sadness at cutting the last ties with his mother and her world. He knew he would never return to Chicago.

The train lurched forward, and John and Rusty smiled at each other as it picked up speed on its journey north. Their thoughts went back almost two years to their first meeting on another northbound train, when they had met by chance and formed a lasting friendship. As the train gathered speed, John took off his coonskin cap and untied his hair. It had been in a ponytail since his return to Chicago and he shook it as it came untied.

"Ah," he said, "that is better. My hair has felt as captive as my spirit since I came to Chicago. I will not miss that town."

"Too crowded for ya, huh?"

"Way too crowded, Rusty. I could stand the noise and smoke, but all those people were just too much for me. I'd rather be caught in a pony stampede than in a crowd of white men."

"You're so right. Those Canadian plains are going to look mighty good to these old eyes."

"You got any plans made, Rusty, after we get up to Saskatchewan Province?"

"Well, first I'm going to visit old Iron Hatchet a spell, just to make sure everything is okay with him. I've heard that the far North Country is really beautiful, and so I might go look around that part of the country for awhile. I'd like to do some trappin' and hunting for beaver pelts. Why don't you come on with me?"

"That sounds real interesting," John answered, watching the lights flash by in the distance, as the sun disappeared below the horizon. "I'd really think about going with you, but I have a wife to consider."

"Well, you think about it," Rusty broke in. "She's a Dakota and been in rougher spots than we'd be in. A gal like Wakala could be a real help to us too, cookin' and sewin' while we was running our trap lines and hunting. From what you've told me about her, she'd be a welcome addition to the long evenings' conversations."

"You really think so?" John asked. "I thought you'd be opposed to having a woman along."

"Where in the hell did you git the idea that I was against women? Why I love 'em all," he shouted, smacking his knee. They laughed as Rusty playfully elbowed John.

"I tell you what," John finally said, "I'll think about it the rest of the trip. Now let me get some sleep while this Iron Horse takes us to Canada."

The balance of the trip was uneventful the train rolled through the countryside of the northern plains. The winter snows were melting, and the grass was turning green and rich, making the journey a pleasant one. They soon left the rail line and headed across country on horseback. It was like old times for them, as they made their way through Canada, camping under the crystal clear skies.

A week had passed when Rusty and John reached the top of a ridge and stopped their horses. John pointed down the valley toward a cabin.

"That's Sergeant Burton's cabin, Rusty."

As they watched, Sergeant Burton appeared on the porch and waved at them. Mounting his black gelding, he rode up the hill to meet them. John thought his friend looked splendid as he approached, wearing a red and gold blazer with an ammunition belt strapped across his chest. The sun reflected brightly off of the Mounties' white gloves.

"Hello, John," Burton called out as they came together about two hundred yards from the cabin.

"Hello, Sergeant Burton," John smiled. "Meet my good friend Rusty Brunner."

The two men shook hands while still on horseback. "Beautiful country you got here, Sergeant!" Rusty exclaimed. "The sky is as clear and blue as God ever made."

"Thank you. We like it too. I'd be glad to show you around sometime if you stay awhile."

The Mountie turned to John, a serious look on his face. "I'm kind of surprised to see you here, John. I take it you didn't get my letter."

"No, I didn't," John answered hesitantly. "Is everything all right with Wakala and the tribe?"

"Well, nobody in Iron Hatchet's tribe has been hurt or anything like that. It's just that they are not here anymore. They moved back to the Dakotas. The game became very scarce and the government cut down on the rations. I tried to fight for the tribe but Ottawa wouldn't listen, insisting that the Hunkpapas were American Indians and not Canadian. Iron Hatchet implored the government to give him permanent land, making a beautiful plea for his people, but the politicians wouldn't change their minds."

"Were they starving?" John interrupted.

"No, nothing that bad, but the lodge kettles were often empty and times were hard. A lot of sickness spread through the camp, making the braves too weak to hunt. On top of that, the winter was a real bad one with blizzards and snowstorms everyday. The Blackfeet shared their rations, but it was making it hard on everyone, and Iron Hatchet knew it.

"Still," John said, "I'm surprised that they left here."

"One other thing decided it, John," the Mountie continued, "some of the young bucks were homesick. They longed to roam the same prairies as their fathers did and fight the Crow."

They reached the little cabin and dismounted. Entering, they sat down while Burton made coffee and continued his story.

"I pleaded with them to stay, as I still had hope of increasing their food rations, but I could not promise them that. I'm only a Mountie, not a politician."

John sat silently, his whole life once again in turmoil. His wife and relatives were now far to the south, living on a strange reservation. He looked at his two friends.

"I'm sure you did your best, Burton. You are a real friend to the Indians. I'm worried about my people once they are in the United States. Perhaps they will be arrested for taking part in the Little Big Horn Massacre."

"Don't worry about that possibility, John. The United States government sent representatives here to talk to them before their return, and Iron Hatchet was promised that they would not be sent to prison for fighting with the Army. I believe them, as the government is anxious to have all the tribes come back to the States. It doesn't look good to have American Indians roaming around free in Canada."

"What reservation were they headed for?" Rusty asked.

"Standing Rock. That's where all the Hunkapapas are supposed to go."

"Do you know if Sitting Bull has gone in?"

"No, he hasn't. As a matter of fact, his tribe just entered Canada and they are going to try to stay here. I'm sure the American government will fight that move, too. They won't be able to leave the greatest living Sioux chief running free in Canada. No, I'm afraid he'll be forced to move back just like Iron Hatchet's band because the Canadian government won't give him any tribal land either."

The three silently sipped their coffee, dreading the thought of the Sioux being forced onto reservations. It would be bad times for a great people.

John turned to Rusty. "Old friend, I'm leaving tomorrow for the Dakotas and my people. I know you wanted to trap in Canada for beaver, so I'll understand if you stay here, but I'd like you to join me, if you would. The two of us working as a team might be able to help the Hunkpapas down on Standing Rock Reservation. After we're there awhile, you could take off again."

"Why, hell yes, I'm going with you," Rusty answered. "Iron Hatchet is a friend and I have to make sure he's okay. Besides, I ain't seen this Wakala gal, yet."

"Sergeant Burton," John asked, "can we spend the night in your cabin?"

"You'd be most welcome. I haven't had any company in a long time. You can fill me in on the news from the civilized world after I fix us some supper."

Chapter Eleven
STANDING ROCK RESERVATION

Reaching down on Panka, Waukesha could feel the sweat and lather caked on his pony's neck. John and Rusty had pushed their horses hard on the ride from Canada, and both the riders and horses were tired and hot.

"Hey, Rusty," he called out to his friend, who was lagging behind. "Let's stop by those oak trees and rest the ponies."

His older partner waved in agreement, and, stopping their horses in the shade, they dismounted to stretch their legs. John sat down on the grass and propped his head against a tree trunk.

"This here Standing Rock sure is a big old place, ain't it, Johnny Boy? Hell, you can ride east clear to the Missouri River before you reach the end of it," Rusty said as he sat next to John.

"Yes, it is big, but once all of the Dakota Territory belonged to my people. Now all we have is this."

"That's true," Rusty said. He pulled out a strand of grass and chewed on it, spitting out the bittersweet juice. "But even at that, the Sioux is luckier than most Indians. They at least got to stay around the bones of their fathers, instead of being shipped down to the Indian Territory. They still have some of their ancestral lands."

"That's so," John answered him, "but look at this land. It is hard. The soil is dry, with barely enough rain to grow a turnip. Yet, the white man expects my people to farm it. Some politician back east decided it was good farmland so, by God, it's good farmland. Only trouble is, they forgot to check and see how little rain we get out here."

"Yeah, but even if it was real good land, the Sioux wouldn't farm it," Rusty interrupted. "Your people consider farming to be woman's work, and no self-respecting brave would be caught dead with a plow in his hand."

John stood up and brushed the dust off his breeches as he climbed upon his pony's back.

"That is the truth, but why should my people be forced to farm just because the white man wants it? We are a free people, born to roam the prairies wherever we want. Farming is for women and white men. The government has taken away our buffalo and now makes us farm in a desert. No wonder we have become beggars. The whites could not defeat us in battle, but they have defeated us on the reservations. A man cannot fight with an empty belly."

Rusty mounted his horse, and they rode silently through the trees along a stream, from which they soon emerged and found a small village of about ten lodges and three cabins below them. The two men rode down the hill into the Dakota village, but no one came out to greet them. The people sat in the dirt by their tipis and watched them pass, their faces tired and drawn.

"Do you recognize any of 'em? I sure don't see anybody I know." Rusty said.

"No, I don't know these people either. I may have met them at the Little Big Horn last year, but they don't look familiar."

As they rode through the village, John could see the tipi hides were showing their age. The hides were torn and faded, as there were no more hunts to obtain new buffalo skins.

A small, black-eyed baby sat in his mother's lap, crying loudly, his stomach swollen from hunger. The child's mother stared at the two riders as she rocked him, trying to stop his wailing. John felt a heavy sorrow in his heart and shook his head sadly.

"Come on, Rusty, let's get out of here." He kicked his pony and the village disappeared in their dust. Up the ridges they raced, trying to leave the poverty and hunger behind them as fast as they could.

"You know, I always loved these old United States," Rusty said when they finally stopped to water their horses. "But I'll be goddamned if I can support a government that deliberately sets out to ruin an entire nation. Hell, those Sioux back there were more like a bunch of lap dogs than the tribe of warriors that I've always known."

"It doesn't sit well with me either. It makes me ashamed of being part white. I hope Iron Hatchet and Wakala are better off than that last village. Let's mount up and maybe we'll find them soon."

As they rode for an hour or so, the green prairie opened up into a valley before. A small stream wound its way through the valley, and a village became visible at the far end. It appeared to be about the size of Iron Hatchet's tribe.

"That's it!" John Waukesha exclaimed. "I can feel it."

He spurred his pony on and they raced along the stream toward the Hunkpapa camp. John pulled away from Rusty and rode swiftly into the village. Much to his dismay, the camp was much like the one they had visited earlier in the day: rotting tipis and strewn garbage. Waukesha saw Iron Hatchet's lance in front of the only wooden building in camp, and he dismounted in front of it. As he did, the cabin door opened and Wakala rushed out, crying.

"Waukesha, my husband, at last you have returned to me. I feared you were killed in Chicago and would never return."

"Of course I came back, Wakala," he said softly, holding her in his arms. "You are my life. My heart ached for you every day while I was gone, for I was like the eagle away from its nest.

"Now, let me look at you."

Wakala stood back from him, tears running down her face. She held his hand tightly.

"What's this?" he asked, patting her belly. "You have put on weight since I left. Is the white man's food so good that Wakala has grown fat?"

Wakala giggled.

"No, silly husband, it is not fat that makes me big. I am carrying the child of my husband, who planted the seed before he left me last winter. I will bear him a fine son soon."

John hugged his wife to him. "Ah, Wakala, that news makes my heart soar with joy. He will be a great Sioux warrior and make us both proud."

As they stood together, Rusty rode up to them and dismounted. He walked over to them and removed his cap.

"Howdy, young lady, you must be Wakala. I'm Rusty Brunner, a friend of John's, and he's told me all about you, but he didn't tell me you was carrying a child. Allow me to congratulate you."

He reached out and shook her hand.

"John Waukesha did not tell you I was with child because he didn't know when he left the land of the Grandmother. I didn't let him know as he had enough worries."

"Well, that sure is good news, Wakala. I hope the child looks like you instead of his father. Nothin' worse than a ugly baby," Rusty laughed. John and Wakala joined in the laughter until Wakala grew serious. She turned to John.

"How was your mother?"

"She is dead. She died during the winter. She had a very happy death, for she was going to meet my father."

"I am sorry," Wakala told him. "Perhaps I will meet her in the next world." They were quite for a moment, not knowing what to say.

Finally Rusty spoke. "How come we ain't seen no braves since we got here?"

"The men have all gone to the agency," Wakala answered. "Today is rations day, so they left early this morning on their buckboards to get our food supplies. I hope the Indian agent gives us all that is ours this month. We are always so hungry and need the food to feed the children. Every ration day the young men get so angry that I am afraid someday there will be a fight with much bloodshed by the Dakotas. I only hope it does not ever come to that.

"But come inside the cabin and rest. Iron Hatchet should be back very soon and will be very happy to see you. If you have any coffee it will give me pleasure to make it for my husband and his good friend."

The afternoon passed in conversation inside the dark cabin. Wakala told John that the conditions on the reservation were extremely bad for the Dakota. The rations were irregular and insufficient, and the Indians had been promised cattle, but never received them. The agent resented Iron Hatchet's authority and tried to deal directly with other tribal members, but the tribe had stuck together so far.

An Indian police force had been formed, and although this sounded like a good idea to John, Wakala assured him it hadn't worked out very well. The Sioux policemen had become tools of the agent, well fed and well armed. They did not hesitate to abuse their authority and were hated by the other Sioux, who called them white man's dogs.

The afternoon was waning when they heard a wagon approaching outside the cabin. John and Rusty ran through the cabin door as Iron Hatchet drove in his buckboard, pulled by two large brown workhorses. Chipeto and Calf Woman sat in the back with the supplies and they started waving wildly at John. Iron Hatchet stopped the horses, and, jumping down, he grasped John in his arms.

"*Hoka Hey!* Calf Woman, come see who has returned to us. Come on, get down here and see how well he looks."

Calf Woman and Chipeto climbed off of the wagon as fast as their heavy bodies would carry them. They were wearing gray cotton dresses and their heads were covered with shawls.

"Hey, Waukesha," Calf Woman called out, "it is time you're returned to us. Your woman is heavy with child and he will need a father. It is good to see you again." Chipeto joined her and the two women hugged John, slapping him on the back in delight.

"Come on," Iron Hatchet said, "let us go into my wooden lodge and talk. The women will unload these few rations the agent saw fit to give us today. I want to hear all about your adventures in Chicago."

Turning to enter the cabin, the old chief greeted Rusty. "Hey, Rusty White Hair, it is good to see Waukesha's friend again. You look as healthy as a buffalo bull."

The three men walked into the cabin and sat at the table while the women carried in the boxes and sat them down in a corner. The boxes contained beans, flour, salt, and other staples. Calf Woman did not bother putting them away, as she would take her supplies directly from the boxes as needed.

How many days' worth of supplies is that?" Rusty asked.

Iron Hatchet laughed loudly. "I know it does not look like much," he answered, "but that is our monthly ration of food. If we ate as often as we are hungry, the food would last only a couple of days. I think the agent is trying to starve us to death. If we all die, than the Great White Father in Washington will no longer have an Indian problem."

John shook his head slowly, remembering back two summers to his first days with the Hunkpapas when all they worried about was riding horses, hunting, and swimming. How could it have gone so bad so quickly? He felt bitterness in his heart toward the American government. No wonder the agent was having trouble with the young men of the tribe.

"Where is Little Horse?" he asked, coming back to reality. "I haven't seen him since we returned."

Iron Hatchet wore a worried look as he answered: "He stayed behind at the ration house. Some young bucks and he got in a bad argument with the agent because he would not give us all of our rations again. The young men became very angry because they know the rations are inside the agent's warehouse but we cannot have them. Only the yellow-dog Indian police saved the agent from being attacked today."

"Why won't he give them out?" John asked.

"I believe he is selling the food to white ranchers and miners. I have never seen him taking the rations, but I have heard the stealing goes on at night and it is the police doing the taking."

"Is there any way you can complain to Washington about this thievery, Chief?" Rusty asked.

"We can talk to Washington only through the agency, so there is no use trying. That is how the agent gets away with starving us. Besides, I don't believe Washington really cares what goes on out here as they are all whites anyway."

Wakala came and stood behind John, placing her hands on his shoulders. He touched her hand lightly.

"What does Little Horse intend to do tonight?" John asked his uncle.

"I do not know. He was so angry. I hope no harm comes to him. He called the Indian police some very bad names today and they were full of hate for him. Perhaps you will ride to the agency, find my son, and bring him home. Little Horse will be so glad to see you that he will return here peacefully. Go, please, and find him for me."

John stood and nodded to the chief. "I'll be happy to go and find my brother, and bring him back to Iron Hatchet's lodge."

"Be careful, John Waukesha," Wakala told him, squeezing his hand.

"You want me to go with you?" Rusty asked.

"No, it would probably be better if you didn't. The Indian police might resent a strange white man sticking his nose in their business."

"You're probably right. I'll just stay here and drink more of Wakala's good coffee with the chief. You watch out for yourself now."

"Don't worry," John called out as he rode off. "I have been away from my wife for too long to do anything foolish."

As John rode the trail toward the agency, the sun was setting on the horizon. Long shadows preceded him as his horse picked her way along the rocky path. Although it was a warm spring evening, John felt very troubled. What kind of a life could he offer his wife and child living on a reservation? Like a caged animal in a zoo? Reservation life was not the Indian life he had grown to love, and he knew his family and people were in for hard times.

After Waukesha had been riding for nearly half an hour, the landscape began to change, becoming hilly with many pine trees. The evening air smelled sweet as darkness set in, and John rode into the blackness of the pine forest. An owl called to him as the moon began to rise, which shed faint light on the dirt road. He let Panka choose her own way to prevent her from tripping in the darkness. The lights of the agency would soon be visible, according to Iron Hatchet's instructions, and then he and Little Horse would be reunited again.

The forest grew very quiet and John reined in his horse to listen. No night noises could be heard, the toads and crickets suddenly silent. He turned his ear toward the trail ahead.

Faintly, he could hear a horse on the soft path. *It's unshod*, he thought, *probably an Indian pony*. John dismounted and led his pony into the pine trees. He whispered into the pony's ear: "Be still, little sister, and we shall see who is coming."

John watched from the trees as the shadowy figure of a rider moved into a clearing. It looked like a young brave on a large pony, and the brave was singing a Dakota tune to his horse as he rode. John recognized the Indian's hat, a U.S. trooper's wide-brimmed hat with an eagle feather in it. It certainly looked like Little Horse.

"Whoa, little warrior!" John cried out from under the pines. "What is a little brave like yourself doing out all alone at night?"

Little Horse stopped his horse and searched the blackness of the trees. The voice had sounded familiar.

"Come out of the darkness," he called back, "and I'll show you how small a warrior that I am. Don't be a rabbit hiding in the bushes."

John crawled out of the trees and jumped up, shouting. "*Hoka Hey*, Cousin, so you have taken to fighting with rabbits now. Well, this rabbit is not afraid."

He ran forward, and, leaping on his cousin's back, they tumbled to the ground. Little Horse rolled on top of John and pinned his shoulders to the wet grass. John squirmed between his cousin's legs, but he could not free himself from the laughing Little Horse. Lifting his legs high, he wrapped them around Little Horse's neck, and, pulling down, he flipped the young Dakota over onto the grass.

They lay there, laughing and breathless.

"Pretty strong rabbit, huh, Little Horse?"

"Very strong, *Hohe*. It makes me feel good to see you again. When did you return to the lodge of Iron Hatchet?"

"Only this afternoon. We were waiting for you when Iron Hatchet started to worry, so he sent me after you."

"No need for my father to worry," Little Horse answered. "The agent finally yielded and issued us additional rations. Now help me pick them up, because you are the reason my food is lying all over the ground. Come on, its only some beans and coffee and the like."

"Are you going to receive the extra rations all the time, or was this an exception?" John asked.

"That I do not know. The agent wasn't going to give us any, but he suddenly changed his mind, probably because he was afraid of us."

The two quickly found the canned goods in the grass and put them into Little Horse's sack.

"Are you staying for good this time, Waukesha?"

"Yes, I am," John answered. "The Dakota are my only people now."

"That is good news. Perhaps with you here, to read the agent's orders and speak his tongue, things will get better for us. He will not be able to cheat us so easily. Anyway, it is great to see you again as I have truly missed my brother."

Little Horse climbed on his pony and looked at the sky. The stars were glistening clearly through the cool air.

"Ah, it is so beautiful now," Little Horse sighed. "One could almost forget the misery of the Dakota people on a night like this. My brother is home and we have food. Perhaps Wakantanka is going to smile on his people yet."

"I am sure he will," John said. "Come, Little Horse, ride up the trail, and I will get my horse from the trees and meet you there. It's time to return to your father's lodge."

Little Horse rode slowly on the trail while John walked into the forest to find his pony. Panka was standing next to the tree where he had left her, and John started to lead her back to the road. Suddenly, the stillness of the night was shattered as two rifle shots were fired in succession. John dropped to the ground instantly. The shots came from up ahead near Little Horse, and John crawled rapidly toward the trail until he could see Swift Moon standing in the moonlight.

"Little Horse," he whispered, "where are you? Are you hurt?"

"Ohh, Waukesha, I am here by my horse. I am badly wounded, my brother. I have been shot."

John crawled onto the path and found his cousin lying under his horse. He slid his hand under Little Horse's head and raised it slightly, blood running down his hand. A hissing sound of air was escaping through the hole in Little Horse's chest.

"Go away, Waukesha," the wounded brave whispered. "I am dead, and you will be killed if you stay here. You cannot help me. I am going to the Spirit World." He coughed weakly.

"Lie still. You are not going to die. I must go kill this dog that shoots in the night, and then I will return for you. Calf Woman and Chipeto will nurse you back to health in no time, and then we will hunt buffalo again. Now, do not move. I will be back soon."

He stripped off his shirt and placed it under Little Horse's bloody head. Although his cousin was still conscious, he did not speak; Waukesha drew his knife and disappeared into the brush on the other side of the rode. Waukesha figured the ambusher would be heading back toward the agency and would have to pass him. Crouching down, he listened for some movement. Nothing. He waited. No sounds. Perhaps he was too late and had missed Little Horse's assassin. A breeze stirred through the pine forest, which caused a chill to pass through his sweaty body. Where was Little Horse's killer?

A slight cracking noise caught his ear. John lay flat on the ground and tried to catch a silhouette against the sky. At last he saw him, an Indian wearing the blue army-type jacket and leggings of the Indian police. He was a big man, but he moved quietly as he headed to his hidden horse.

Waukesha slipped down into a gully and crawled on his belly ahead of the Indian policeman to a rock formation. He scrambled up on the rocks and waited for his foe to walk under him. His heart pounding loudly, John jumped, shouting at the top of his lungs. He landed on the policeman's back and brought his knife down hard into the man's stomach. The Indian screamed in pain, his rifle firing wildly as John plunged the knife in his chest, his side, and finally his neck. Blood flowed freely, covering John's hands and arms. He stabbed the policeman once more and let him fall to the forest floor, his life flowing from him. John stood over him, a feeling of great joy coming over him.

"Sing your death song, Brother," he shouted. "At least die like a true Dakota."

The dying policeman moved his mouth as if to sing, but no sound came out of his slashed throat. He looked at John and fell back as his spirit left him.

John bent down, took his knife, and cleanly lifted the dead man's scalp. He held the hair up to the sky.

"You do not deserve to enter the next world with your hair, low dog. You have shot one of your brothers for the white man, and all our dead brothers will know what you have done. I will give your hair to Little Horse so he will know you have paid for your cowardly deed."

He sat the body up and pulled it over his shoulder. Standing with a grunt, John shifted the body so he could walk. He carried the dead Indian down the slope of a hill to a small creek, where he walked in the stream's icy water for about one hundred feet. John had trouble breathing, for the slain Sioux had been a large man. Finally, he reached a spot where there were many boulders, and he rolled the corpse off his shoulders onto the ground. Waukesha turned the police man on his back and began piling stones on the body. It was very quiet; only the clacking of rocks could be heard as John covered the dead man. He piled the stones quickly, for he knew Little Horse was badly wounded and needed him. Cutting down several small branches, Waukesha placed them over the grave, and then tossed the policeman's rifle into the thick underbrush.

Satisfied with his work, he started running through the trees toward Little Horse. Stumbling over roots and branches, he fell twice, cutting his arm as he crashed into a tree stump. The pain throbbed in his arm, but he continued running up the hillside until the trail was visible in the moonlight.

"Little Horse!" he called out, as he ran on the trail. "I'm coming back. Are you all right?"

No answer came back.

"Little Horse?" he cried again as he saw his cousin laying on the trail in the same spot where he had been shot. John knelt down and lifted his cousin's head. The wounded brave slowly opened his eyes.

"Have you slain the rattlesnake that killed me?" Little Horse whispered.

"Yes, I have. It was a Sioux policeman, and he will enter the Happy Hunting Grounds without his hair."

"That is good," Little horse said, a weak smile on his lips. "Come closer to me." He took John's hand. "I am dying, *Hohe*, and you cannot save me."

John moved to speak in protest, but Little Horse signaled him to stop.

"Do not weep for me," the dying brave continued, speaking very softly, "for it will be a better place for the Dakota where I am going. I will be free again like when you and I were camped on the Little Turnip Creek. In those days, one Dakota would not kill another."

He stopped talking to breathe, his chest heaving up and down.

"Tell my father," Little Horse gasped, "that I died like a Hunkpapa brave. Tell him we will hunt together again in the next world. You will be with us, Brother, and we will all be free again to hunt the buffalo and to raid the Crows.

"Tell him I…"

Little Horse tried to continue talking, but he could form no words. He grasped at John's hand. Little Horse groaned quietly and his body suddenly went limp. He released John's hand as his spirit left him for the next world.

John held his dead cousin's head in his hands, the bitter tears flowing down his face. Stroking Little Horse's face, he wiped the dirt off and closed his eyes. He sat, holding his cousin, as his mind roamed back over the past two years and the times the two of them had shared. Seldom were two men as close as they had been, and now it had come to an end. He felt despair welling up within him.

"Oh, God," he sobbed. "Will we all end up like this?"

The minutes passed slowly in the dark woods as the night sounds returned. Crickets chirped loudly, and John realized he could hear a frog down by the creek. John touched the face of Little Horse gently. He had been such a true friend. Standing up, he cradled his cousin in his arms. He carried him to Swift Moon, and draped Little Horse over the pony's back.

"Walk smoothly, Swift Moon," he said, patting the pony. "Your master cannot hold on this night. Do not let him fall in the dirt again."

John cried as he led Panka to the road and slid onto her back. Bending over, he grasped the reins of Swift Moon and nudged his pony forward, wiping the tears from his eyes. He did not try to stop the tears. He was not afraid to cry over the death of Little Horse.

The two horses moved slowly along the dusty trail, as if they too felt the sorrow John possessed. As he rode, holding the reins of Swift

Moon, Waukesha looked at the sky and prayed to Wakantanka. He prayed for Little Horse, but mostly he prayed for the Dakota people. It seemed to him that the Great Spirit had deserted them, and they were all destined to be destroyed. He prayed hard while he rode in the darkness, hoping that the Dakota people would survive.

Iron Hatchet and Rusty stood in front of the lodge, watching as a rider approached, leading another slow-moving pony on the dark trail. The moonlight bathed the young rider, whose head was bowed low as the horses entered the village. The two men could see the second horse was carrying a body.

"It is John Waukesha who rides sitting up," Iron Hatchet said. "He is much thinner than Little Horse."

"You're right, Chief," Rusty agreed. "It's John all right. C'mon, let's go see what happened."

They rushed down the trail to meet John. "You okay?" Rusty asked him.

John nodded.

"Is that Little Horse on the pony?" the large man asked, as he helped him off Panka.

"Yes, Rusty, it is my dead brother, my *hohe*."

Iron Hatchet walked around to the second horse and lifted his son's head to look at his face. The old chief's face showed no emotion as he lowered the head, and turned to the crowd that had gathered.

"Go back to your tipis, my people. You cannot help Little Horse anymore. He has joined Wakantanka. Go now."

The chief looked very old to John as he talked to his people, his shoulders slouched deeply. The tribal members slowly walked away, leaving the three of them alone with the body of Little Horse.

"Who has killed my son, Waukesha?" Iron Hatchet asked, looking into John's eyes.

John fought the dryness in his throat, finding it difficult to talk about his cousin's death. "An Indian policeman shot him from the trees as we rode the trail back to your camp. Little Horse never saw him."

"Did you see him, Waukesha?"

"I did better than that. I chased the policeman, killed him, and took his scalp. He will slay no more Dakota brothers. I have avenged my brother's death, but it will not bring Little Horse back to us. He has gone to Wakantanka and we will not see him for many winters. He said to tell you that he will hunt with you again when you join him."

Iron Hatchet put his hand on John's shoulders. "You have once again proven yourself to be a true Dakota. Your deeds will help console me when I think of Little Horse. He was a fine son that would have made any Dakota proud to be his father.

"Now I will carry him to my lodge, and we will bury him tomorrow when the sun rises. Calf Woman will want to dress him in his best buckskin tonight."

The chief gently slipped his son's body off the horse into his arms, and walked effortlessly to the cabin, disappearing inside. John and Rusty walked slowly toward the corral, leading the horses.

"I reckon you better git in the cabin and see your woman," Rusty told him after a moment. "Wakala's been worried sick about you bein' gone so long and all. I'll take care of these horses. You probably need a rest after the night you've had."

"Thank you, friend. I don't believe I've ever felt this tired." John slowly walked to the cabin and opened the door. Wakala rushed to him and held him tight. His tears started again. Between sobs, he told her the long, sad story of Little Horse's death.

Rusty led the ponies around to the rail and brush corral behind the cabin. He turned the horses loose inside and sat on the ground, leaning against a post. Eventually he dozed off, sleeping fitfully on the earth through the remains of the night.

As dawn lit the eastern sky, Rusty woke to see John and Iron Hatchet standing in front of the cabin. They were wrapped in army blankets against the morning chill as they talked quietly, obviously trying not to wake the women inside.

"I been wantin' to talk to you two," Rusty said, as he joined them.

"Chief, we got to be thinking about old Johnny Boy's safety, you know. The police will find that body this morning and they'll be here looking for someone to pay the piper. I think we ought to be gittin' the hell out of here, pronto."

"No, I won't leave yet," John said. "I will not go until my brother is buried. Besides, I hid the policeman's body so well they will not find it too quickly."

Iron Hatchet listened to both of them, the sorrow showing in his eyes. His voice quivered slightly as he spoke.

"Your white haired friend is right, Waukesha. You can no longer stay here at Standing Rock with us. The dog police will kill you just like they killed Little Horse, and then Wakala will be a widow again. Still, I will not make you leave until we have given Little Horse a proper funeral."

"Thank you, Uncle. I will leave by noon today, so they will not catch me. It will make my heart heavy to leave my people again."

"Come on then," Rusty butted in, "let's get on with it and build Little Horse a first class funeral scaffold. It won't do him any good if John gets killed while we stand around talkin'."

The three men walked behind the cabin into the small stand of growing cottonwoods. Iron Hatchet selected four trees that were like the corners of a rectangle, and John chopped away the brush growing around the trunks. After Rusty cut some willow saplings, they made a scaffold, tying the ends together to make a firm bed for Little Horse.

The sun was above the trees when the funeral procession finally began. John carried one end of the scaffold and Iron Hatchet the other. Iron Hatchet was wearing his best blue trousers and deerskin shirt, and on his head was his war bonnet with hundreds of eagle feathers trailing to the ground. Little Horse lay on the scaffold, dressed in buckskin trousers and his blue cavalry shirt, his face painted in white and red stripes, while a blue beaded headband held an eagle feather in place.

His bow rested on top of him, as were a pair of army boots he had won at the Little Big Horn.

A medicine man walked along with the funeral, chanting and shaking a rattle made from a turtle shell. He was wearing a large gold medallion, and he wailed to the Great Spirit as they walked, praying for the soul of Little Horse. Calf Woman, Chipeto, and Wakala walked last, keening loudly and beating their breasts. Following them were the friends of Little Horse: young braves, old men, and children of the tribe.

As the small procession moved out of the cabin and around the corral to the cottonwoods, the three women cried even louder, joined by many others in the crowd. The medicine man shouted his prayers to the heavens until the procession halted by the four cottonwoods. John and Iron Hatchet raised the body and placed the scaffold in the trees. John tied rawhide around Little Horse's body and secured it to the trees so it would not be blown out.

Reaching up, he touched the hand of Little Horse. "Have a good journey, Brother. We shall ride the wind together someday."

He placed the dead policeman's scalp on Little Horse's chest, and, turning away, he walked into the pine forest to be alone. Tears flowed freely down his cheeks.

Chapter Twelve
THE ESCAPE

It was noon on the day of the funeral, and Iron Hatchet carried Wakala's bedding out of the cabin, where he placed it in the back of his wagon. The wagon bed already contained boxes of canned goods and blankets, covered up by Waukesha's buffalo robe. Iron Hatchet laid the bedding down neatly, near the sideboards, so Wakala could rest on the long journey to the safety of Canada. He looked up as Wakala walked out of the cabin carrying two baskets. She handed them to him, and he put them in the front under the buffalo robe. Sitting down on the end of the wagon, he patted her hand.

"You have been very much like a daughter to me, Wakala," he told her. "I shall miss your beautiful smile around my lodge."

"I will miss you also, Uncle. I have grown very fond of Chipeto, Calf Woman, and you. You have cared for me like I was your own."

Iron Hatchet stood up to walk back into the cabin, but he stopped and spoke again. "Do not let him return to this place once you have escaped here, Wakala. Waukesha will not be safe here ever, for the agent will have his revenge. You must try to make him forget us, and make a new life for yourselves in the Grandmother's land."

"We will never forget you," she said. "He is like your son, and we are Hunkpapas. We do not leave our parents out of our hearts when they grow old. No, we shall always miss you, but I will keep him away from Standing Rock. There is nothing for us here but trouble."

John and Rusty interrupted them as they emerged from the cabin. The two friends looked solemn as they walked up to the chief and Wakala.

"Are you ready to go?" Iron Hatchet asked.

"Yes," John answered. "We are loaded, but I still feel like I am deserting my people. I should be here to help fight for the Dakota's lands and freedom."

"You are right, of course, but when they hang you for murdering a policeman, what good will that do anyone? You will be dead, Wakala will be a widow, and there will be one less Sioux for the whites to worry about."

"The chief is absolutely right," Rusty butted in. "I'm surprised they haven't been here yet lookin' for that police's killer. C'mon, John, quit arguing and let's git going. I don't aim to stand around here until you're caught and hanged."

John took a deep breath and looked into Wakala's eyes. He nodded his head. "Let's go then."

"Wakala climb in the buckboard, while I ride Panka to look out for the Sioux police. Rusty will you drive the team?"

"Sure, Johnny Boy."

"Wait," Iron Hatchet said. "I have something for you, Waukesha." The old chief disappeared behind the cabin and soon emerged, leading the brown and white pinto Swift Moon by the reins. He handed them to John.

"Take him my son," the chief told John. "He should be owned by a young and free brave, not an old reservation chief like myself."

159

"But he is the pony of Little Horse, "John protested. "He belongs to you."

"Yes he does, so I can give him away if I want. Little Horse would smile if he knew you were taking Swift Moon. Take him or I will have to sell him for food or medicine, and some white man will end up with him."

"Thank you, Iron Hatchet," John said, taking the reins. "He is a fine gift. Now I have a gift for you."

He reached in the saddlebags of Rusty's horse and pulled out a package wrapped in brown paper. He handed it to Iron Hatchet.

"What is it?" Iron Hatchet asked.

"It is the white man's money. It is over five hundred dollars, and it will help to buy many rations and medicine for my people. Take it to the Quakers who live near the Standing Rock agency. You can trust them, and they will help you use it wisely. Do not tell anyone else you have it as it is a good deal of money, and they would kill you for it. Especially do not let the agent or police know you have it."

"I understand," the chief answered, sticking the package inside his shirt. "I will take it to the Quakers before the sun sets today. It will be a great help for my people."

John hugged the old man to him. "Thank you for everything. Perhaps we shall meet again someday where all men will be brothers."

"Perhaps we shall, Waukesha."

Rusty shook the old man's hand. "So long, Chief. Take care of yourself and those women of yours."

"Take care of my son, White Hair. You are a wise white man and real friend," Iron Hatchet said, shaking Rusty's hand firmly.

Wakala sat waiting patiently in the back of the wagon. She waved sadly to Calf Woman and Chipeto, who were standing in the doorway. Rusty climbed into the driver's seat of the wagon while John tied Panka and Rusty's horse to the rear end. He then climbed on Swift Moon's back, setting the rifle he had taken from the Ree across his lap.

"So long, Calf Woman and Chipeto. May Wakantanka smile on you. Goodbye, Iron Hatchet."

He kicked the pony and they rode slowly out of the village up the ridge. John looked back at the cabin with Little Horse's funeral scaffold behind it. He could still see the women waving at him as once again he left his people. He felt sad—his heart felt heavy as they rode down the hill. Iron Hatchet's camp soon disappeared below the ridgeline.

Iron Hatchet also rode from the village after John departed. He rode hard for the Quaker's missionary. There, he entrusted the money with Friend Taylor, who ran the church. He was an honest white man who would spend the money for the chief to buy needed supplies.

This money lasted for over two years, and helped many reservation Indians survive those first difficult times.

Returning in the late afternoon, Iron Hatchet was dismayed to see five Indian police standing under the funeral scaffold of Little Horse. They were questioning Calf Woman and Chipeto, but the two women would not answer them, only crying louder and louder at each question. Iron Hatchet smiled proudly at this game his wives were playing with the policemen.

He rode up to them and dismounted, releasing his pony into the corral. One Bull, a large ugly man who was especially disliked by the Dakotas, led the group of police. One Bull signaled the chief to come over to them, but he did not move from the corral railing.

"Come over here and we shall talk, One Bull," Iron Hatchet called out. "Have you lost your respect for the dead since you have become the agent's policeman? You are still a Dakota. Now move away from my son's body and we shall talk."

Looking somewhat embarrassed by this public chastisement, One Bull led his men away from the scaffold of trees to the aging chief. They wore the blue policeman's uniform with black fur caps, and all carried repeating rifles. The Sioux policemen formed a circle around the chief, while Calf Woman and Chipeto ran into the safety of the cabin.

"How did your son die?" One Bull asked.

"I do not know, One Bull," Iron Hatchet answered. "He was shot in the back late last night as he returned from the agency with some extra rations. I found him dead on his pony this morning. He was probably killed by some white man."

"He was not killed by white men, Chief, and you know it. He was killed while being chased by an Indian policeman because he stole those extra rations."

"You are a liar, One Bull," the Chief angrily spat out. "My son was no thief. He was given those rations so your men would have a reason to ambush him."

One Bull's face was livid with rage. He raised his arm as if to strike Iron Hatchet, but slowly lowered it as he pushed down the anger.

"Your son was a thief, and he has been dealt with like all thieves," One Bull shouted at the chief. "But now there is a police murderer loose in your village. We want him."

"Who was murdered?" Iron Hatchet asked innocently.

"Okay, Iron Hatchet, I will play your childish game if you want. One of my best men, Lame Fox, was murdered last night after he shot Little Horse. It is his murderer I want."

About twenty-five braves, who had been watching the entire scene, now surrounded the group. Several of the men carried knives, and they were ready to spring on the agency policemen if Iron Hatchet called on them.

"Are you accusing me, One Bull?" Iron Hatchet finally said. "I was here all night, as my people will tell you. Perhaps Little Horse killed the snake before he died."

"No, he did not. Lame Fox was killed, carried very far, and buried under a pile of stones. Your son could not have done that after being seriously wounded. And you did not kill him either, Iron Hatchet. But we have heard of a visitor you had yesterday, a young Dakota brave from Canada. I believe he was your nephew and the husband of Wakala."

"I don't have any nephews. My only brother was killed many summers back, and the Crows stole his son. I have no nephew that I know of."

"You are lying," One Bull said, pushing his way to the corral. "Where is your wagon, old man?"

Iron Hatchet hesitated for an instant. "One of my warriors borrowed it to go to the agency this morning."

"Ha, that is a poor story for so wise a man," One Bull said, laughing. "So your nephew took the wagon. That is why I have not seen Wakala around your lodge today. She is too heavy with child to ride a pony, and the wagon's trail will be easy enough to find. Come, men, mount up and let's go after them."

By this time, the crowd had moved between the police and their horses. They stood firm as the policemen started walking toward them.

"Cock your rifles!" One Bull shouted to his policemen. "Iron Hatchet, move your people or someone will get killed, and it won't be my men. Now move them."

Iron Hatchet walked in front of the armed policemen and spoke to his people.

"Thank you for your support, my people. You have made my heart proud with your Dakota bravery. But, let these men pass through or they will start shooting, and our children may be hurt. Let them pass. They will not catch our brother Waukesha for he is a Hunkpapa, and these white men's dogs will never find him."

He walked into the crowd and pushed them back to form a passage for the five men. The Indian police moved through the crowd and quickly mounted.

From his horse, One Bull threatened Iron Hatchet: "We shall see who is a real man, Iron Hatchet, when we find this Waukesha and bring his hair back to you. Then you will see how we treat those who attack the Standing Rock police."

They kicked the sides of their horses and thundered out of the village, dust swirling high behind them.

The fugitives had set a brisk pace during the early afternoon to put as much distance between them and the agency police as they could. It was a long ride before they would be safely off of the Standing Rock reservation. The sun fell below the ridgeline as they stopped to rest near a small stream. Wakala soon fell asleep on the wagon, secure in the company of her husband and his large white friend.

Rusty turned to John and whispered. "We gotta make some plans now before we leave this place, Johnny Boy. This here wagon is leaving a trail like a herd of buffalo for them policemen to follow, and we got to do somethin' about it."

"You're right, Rusty," John said. "Do you have a plan in mind? Unless I'm mistaken, my guess is that you've got this whole thing plotted out."

Rusty smiled broadly and squeezed John's shoulder firmly with his hand.

"You're gettin' awful smart," Rusty said, grinning. "Now, here's how I figger we can fool 'em, but we need Wakala's help."

He looked at Wakala, who had sat up when the two started talking. Wrapping her blanket around her against the chill, she climbed down from the wagon and walked over to lean against John. "I will be glad to help my husband," she said clearly.

"Good," Rusty said. "I know'd you was a good woman.

"Now, what we got to do is keep them on the trail of the wagon while you two is ridin' horseback off of this reservation. I'll drive the wagon with my horse pulling along behind it, so's I can join up with you later. What do you say, Wakala. Can you ride alright?"

"I am able to ride, White Hair. I am not so pregnant as to hurt the child I bear, but we will have to ride slowly.

"But what about you? What will the police do to you when they find out John is not with the wagon? Will you be arrested?"

"Don't worry about me none, little one," Rusty answered with a wave of his arm. "I'm a white man; they won't mess with me. It's John they want, and they'll be after him as fast as they can. No need to worry about old Rusty."

John had remained silent through most of this conversation. He looked up and could see the sky had turned slightly lighter. "I think it is a good plan. The agency police are surely on our trail by now, and they will catch us all in the wagon if we stay with it. We will ride Panka and Swift Moon as fast as we safely can to the north, while you head west. If we are lucky, Wakala and I will be off of the reservation by sundown today, and then we will slow down so you can catch up with us."

"That's good thinkin'," Rusty agreed. "I'll hook up my horse to the wagon and be on my way."

"Good luck," John called out. "We will ride up the creek until we can lose our tracks on the rocks. We'll see you tonight."

"See you later," Rusty shouted as he lashed the team, and they trotted briskly across the plains, the wagon bouncing behind them.

One Bull and the agency policemen had not stopped to rest at sundown, but continued on the trail, following the ruts left by the wagon in the dark. It was slow moving and required frequent stops to find the trail, but they were gaining on the fugitives. One Bull hoped to find them in camp and ambush them while they slept. Bear's Robe, a young Minneconjou Sioux who had joined the police for some excitement, was doing the actual tracking. With war parties and buffalo hunting a thing of the past, there wasn't much for a young man to do on the reservation, and Bear's Robe had hoped to win some glory on the police force. Still, as he followed the trail, he wasn't sure that pursuing other Dakotas was what he had in mind when he joined.

Bear's Robe rode on ahead of the others, and he found where Waukesha's group had stopped to rest. He dismounted and studied the pony tracks carefully.

Something was not right. One of the two ponies that had been pulled along behind the wagon was not there when the wagon left the camp. He searched the creek bed until he found two different hoof marks. The young Sioux knew Waukesha and his wife had left the wagon and gone their own way.

He sat down by the stream, troubled. Little Horse had always been a friend to him, and his murder had shocked him. Now his job was to find the cousin of Little Horse and probably kill him, too. Instead of helping his people as he had hoped, he was now killing them off like a white man.

It was light now, and he could see the Indian police approaching him slowly, three of the braves sleeping in the saddle. Bear's Robe mounted his pony and rode up to them, calling out to One Bull as he pulled to a stop.

"They camped here last night, Sergeant One Bull, but we are too late. They have set out already, heading west."

"What of the one on the horse?" One Bull asked. If he was disappointed in not finding them asleep, he did not show it.

"He has ridden off along the ridges to the south," Bear's Robe answered. "But I am sure he only scouts for us and will rejoin them up ahead."

John and Wakala covered much ground in the morning, but the hot afternoon sun had taken its toll on Wakala. She was tiring, and they were forced to stop and rest several times. Their pace was now very slow, and, as the sun touched the prairies' horizon, John knew that sundown would find them hours from the reservation's border to face another dangerous night. John slowed Swift Moon until he was even with Wakala. Reaching over, he took her hand.

"How are you feeling?"

"Oh, I will be fine, husband," she answered weakly. "Do not worry, as I am only a little tired. Ride on and we shall soon be safe, and then I will sleep like a baby."

He squeezed her hand firmly and patted her belly. "We can ride a short time longer and then find a campsite for tonight. I don't believe the police will catch up with us after the chase Rusty has given them. Perhaps they gave up after they found him. Ride on slowly now while I go up this ridge to scout behind us."

He pulled the reins to the side and turned Swift Moon toward the ridge. Suddenly, a rifle shot rang out from the hill. Panka shuddered slightly and dropped to her knees, a large red spot flowing onto the pony's gray chest. She rolled over, almost gently, throwing Wakala to the ground. Another shot smacked the grass by Swift Moon. John jumped off and ran over to his wife. She lay on her back feeling her stomach to make sure the baby was all right.

"Are you hurt?" he asked, scanning the hills for the ambushers.

"I am fine," she whispered.

"Are you sure?" he asked, his heart pounding wildly. "Can you stand? You must run into those oak trees, or we will both be killed. They have decided I will make a better prisoner as a dead man."

He helped her to her feet as two more bullets sprayed the ground around them. "Take the reins of Swift Moon and run as fast as a deer for the trees."

She did as she was told, without question. John crawled back over to Panka's body and lay down behind the horse while Wakala ran across the field. He patted the dead pony. "I am sad to lose you, Panka. A Dakota could not ask for a better pony."

He watched the hilltop carefully until he saw the smoke from a rifle shot. He laid his rifle barrel across the dead pony's belly and aimed. He squeezed off a shot, hitting just below the hidden policeman. The others opened fire as bullets whizzed by John, striking Panka and the dirt behind him. With shots firing wildly, John tried to pin them down long enough for Wakala to make her escape. He quickly fired four rounds as Wakala disappeared into the trees.

Stripping off his shirt, he threw it over the horse's body. Several shots rang out from behind the bushes and boulders of the ridge, and John saw there were at least four policemen above him. They had him pinned down, but they would soon have to come down for him as darkness was only an hour away, and he could disappear into the night. Minutes passed and no shots were fired. *They are forming their plans*, he thought. *Well, I am ready. If they kill me, they will know they have been in a fight.*

After reloading his rifle, he jumped up from behind Panka, shouting Hunkpapa war whoops as he rushed across the twenty yards of buffalo grass toward the large boulders at the base of the hill. Bullets whizzed by him, but his medicine was strong and he was not hit. John dove behind the rocks, sliding on his chest and hands.

"Hey, low-dogs!" he shouted. "You shoot like Crow women. Did the white agent teach you how to shoot?"

"We shall see who is the old woman before this day is over!" one of the policemen yelled back. The policeman who yelled raised himself just slightly, and John saw his head rise above the rocks. Waukesha propped his elbow against the boulder and sighted on the trooper. Squeezing off the shot, the policeman's head vanished simultaneously with a scream. John crouched down again behind his cover, and he decided to let the agency police make the next move.

Up on the hill, One Bull crawled over to the body of Owl's Foot. The brave lay dead on the rocks where Waukesha's bullet had smashed into his brain, which killed him instantly. One Bull removed Owl's Foot's ammunition belt and picked up his rifle from the crevasse where it had fallen.

"You were a stupid man, Owl's Foot," he muttered as he walked away from the body toward his other two men who waited for their orders in the rocks. Earlier, before the police were in place for the ambush, Owl's Foot had been the one who had opened fire on Waukesha and his wife. They had ridden hard just to catch the fugitives, and One Bull had deployed his men when Owl's Foot had started shooting. If he had waited, One Bull and the three policemen probably would have killed Waukesha and Wakala in the first attack. Now they had to flush Waukesha out and kill him.

It had been a bad day for One Bull and his policemen. They had chased the wagon until noon before they finally caught it, only to find it driven by some strange white man. This white haired giant would tell them nothing. He was obviously used to decoy them from Waukesha's trail and tried to stall them, but One Bull was determined to catch the young renegade. He had to show Iron Hatchet who really ran the reservation. He had wanted to punish this white man, but he feared for his life if he harmed any white man. They had turned northeast, hoping to cut off the fugitives before they reached the reservation border.

One Bull did not believe Bear's Robe had not noticed the missing pony's tracks behind the wagon, so he had sent him back to the agency. He would be no help on this assignment, and One Bull would deal with him harshly when they returned to Standing Rock. Now, he needed a good plan to kill off this young brave pinned down below them in the rocks and shrubs.

He squatted down between his two remaining policemen, and, drawing with a stick in the dirt, he showed them what to do. They should each work down the side of the hill, trapping Waukesha in the middle of a triangle. One Bull would fire down on the brave to cover their movements until they were in position behind the huge boulders on each side of the Hunkpapa. Then, One Bull would crawl down the hill to close in the pincers and kill him.

The two men studied the drawings in the dirt and nodded in understanding. The sun was low in the sky and would make it difficult for Waukesha to see them, as he was looking directly into its burning rays. The policemen felt it was a good plan, and, crouching low behind the rocks, they disappeared over the hillside. As One Bull lay on the rocks, he peered slowly down the hill to where the young Hunkpapa was trapped. He watched the two policemen working their way cautiously down the hill, darting from rock to rock, then behind an occasional pine tree, always closing in on Waukesha.

One Bull did not only watch them, though. His eyes scanned across the whole scene until he saw a slight movement in the rocks. It was Waukesha aiming his rifle at the policeman moving down on his right. One Bull squeezed the trigger as the Indian's black hair rose just above the rocks. The bullet smashed into the rock, sending splinters flying as the head disappeared in the smoke.

"Haa!" One Bull shouted. "I think I got him! But be careful as he may only be fooling us like the possum." The two braves smiled at this encouraging news and quickened their pace.

John had not been hit directly by One Bull's bullet, but several rock splinters had hit him in the forehead, which knocked him on the ground and momentarily stunned him. He lay on his back feeling his bloodied forehead. Luckily, the splinters missed his eyes; otherwise, his life would have soon been over. He sat up and wiped the blood from his face on his buckskin trousers. Shaking his head, he grabbed his rifle from the weeds and crawled back behind his rock.

Waukesha knew he was in trouble. The two policemen were now down on the valley floor, level with his position, and would soon have him in a deadly crossfire. If he had ever been in a tighter spot, he couldn't remember when.

He pushed himself against the boulders. He decided to charge the policeman on the right, kill him, and then escape into the trees beyond the rocks. John realized he would probably be killed first, but he saw no other choice. His heart pounding, he fired two quick shots at the policeman's hiding place to pin him down. Waukesha then jumped up and ran toward him as a bullet tore into the grass beneath his feet, spitting dirt. He dove into the high grasses and rolled down the hill, bullets kicking all around him. John stopped rolling next to a pine tree where he slid around its trunk and aimed his rifle into the trees just twenty yards in front of him. A flash of uniform blue came through the green grass and John fired, the rifle cracking loudly. A scream came from his enemy as the policeman crashed through the trees and fell face down on the rocks. He grasped his leg in pain, wounded badly.

John turned quickly around the tree to look for the other two above him. He saw One Bull kneeling openly on the rocks, his rifle aimed at John. A shot rang out, but John did not feel it hit him nor did it smack the tree in front of him. Instead, One Bull slowly crumbled over as his rifle slipped from his hands and slid down the rocks, bouncing wildly until it came to rest on the grass. The police leader rolled on his back and slid down slowly behind his rifle. His arms were outstretched below him, and, to John, he looked like a great snake sliding down the hillside.

The hilltop was now occupied by One Bull's killer, a large man, standing in the blinding sun. John could hardly identify him. He carried a rifle, which was not aimed at John but toward the only remaining policeman. His voice boomed down to Waukesha.

"You okay, Johnny Boy?"

"Yes, I'm fine," John called back as he recognized Rusty's voice.

"Good. I was afraid I might've been too late when I heard all the shootin' going on. I reckon I got here just in time 'cause I believe that damn old sergeant's bullet had your name on it."

"I think you're right, Rusty," John shouted, still squinting up into the sun. "What happened to the other policeman?"

Rusty started laughing.

"Hell, don't you worry about that other one. He saw which way the wind was blowing and lit out of here quick as a mule deer. By the time old One Bull had stopped sliding, that other boy was runnin' hard for Standing Rock. You just stay where you are. I'm coming down."

John watched him climb down the hill, moving with remarkable grace. Rusty stopped by One Bull and slung the dead leader's body over his shoulder, continuing on effortlessly. Reaching John and the wounded Sioux, he laid the body down and John hugged the old man.

"Thank you again, my friend," John told him. "You have saved my life."

Rusty pushed him away gently.

"Oh hell, it wasn't nothin' I did. You'd a done the same for me," he muttered. Rusty suddenly realized Wakala was missing.

"Where's that pretty little wife of yours? She ain't hurt is she?"

"No, she's fine. She's hiding in those trees across the valley floor. I am sure she has seen all of this and is feeling better now."

"That's good," Rusty said. "C'mon now, we better get a move on. Let's bandage up this here fella you wounded, and we'll let him take his sergeant's body back to the agent. By the time they come lookin' for us, we'll be clear up into Canada."

"Where are their ponies? They killed Panka and we will need an extra one."

"They're up on the other side of the hill," Rusty answered. "And I guess there is an extra one since that fella lying dead up in those rocks won't be needing his.

"I'll go fetch their horses and bring 'em back here. I can patch up this wounded fella good enough so he can ride back to Standing Rock without bleedin' to death. You better go make sure Wakala is okay and I'll join you in a shake."

Rusty walked over the ridge as he continued talking. He didn't really care if John could hear him anymore; he often talked just for the sound of his voice. John smiled as he could still hear Rusty talking after he disappeared behind the rocks.

It had been a lucky day on that train from Chicago when the big mountain man chose the seat next to him.

John looked across the valley as Wakala emerged from the trees, leading Swift Moon. He waved to her and she answered him with a wave. Running down the hill, he past Panka's body as he crossed the valley and reached for his wife.

"*Hoka Hey*! Wakala!" he shouted, embracing her. "We have made it. No one will catch us now. Soon we will be in Canada where we can be free."

She clung tightly to his bare chest, tears streaming down her face. She looked up in his eyes. "I was so afraid watching you from the trees, Waukesha," she sobbed. "I thought you would be killed and our son would never see you."

"It looked pretty bad, but it's all over now. Rusty has proven himself again, and we will all soon be safe in Canada."

"He must always stay with us," Wakala said. "His medicine is strong."

"I am sure we can convince him to stay with us," John told her. "He will be a part of our new life in Canada.

"Come on, he's bringing the horses. We need to ride a little while until we find a good place to camp for tonight. Then, tomorrow we shall enter the Grandmother's Land."

She slipped her blanket over John's bare shoulder, and, taking Swift Moon by the reins, she and John walked down the slope to meet Rusty.

Chapter Thirteen
CANADA

The snow lay heavy on the pine trees that surrounded John's farm. There had been a freezing rain two days earlier, followed by eight inches of driving snow, which had bent many jack pines low to the ground. The trees formed a half circle, bringing the fresh branches down where the half-starved deer would feed on them. Deer could be found standing on their hind legs, eating off these bent over pines, as soon as the icy northern blasts subsided. Since this was their only food source in hard times, they would often strip the trees completely.

John Waukesha Holcumb was well aware of the mule deer's feeding habits, and his knowledge was rewarded this bright morning. As he rode Swift Moon slowly through the deep snow, a large buck was tied across the pony's back. The venison would be a welcome addition to his family's diet, and the deerskin would be made into a shirt and trousers for his son Little Frog. John grinned as he thought of the four-year old boy. He was a fine young Dakota, full of life and mischief, always off in the woods or down by the river trying to catch some small animal. Little Frog would keep them for a few days and then return them to the wild. In that way, the boy was very much like his uncle Little Horse had been in his youth.

The trail grew steeper, and John dismounted. The snow had blown into deep drifts during the blizzard, and he had to help pull Swift Moon to the top of the ridge.

"C'mon boy," he called, pulling on the bridle. The horse struggled through the belly-high drifts, breathing harder as he jumped forward and sank into the snow. John stopped pulling and let the horse rest.

"Take it easy, Swift Moon. You're not a colt anymore. We have only a little way to go to the top where it will be much easier traveling. It's all down hill from there to the corral and your feed."

They resumed their struggle until the drifts were behind them, and they stood breathlessly on the summit of the ridge. Below them lay the homesteads of John Holcumb and Rusty Brunner. Together, the claims gave them two thousand acres, which would all pass to John and his family when Rusty died. It was their claim to a share of the Canadian wilderness, which would be theirs forever.

This arrangement of side-by-side cabins, which Sergeant Burton had helped cut through the bureaucratic red tape, gave them control of the whole valley where John was standing. It was largely tree-covered hills, rolling down to the flat valley and stream, which sliced through it. The river looked like a blue ribbon lying loosely on a white veil. John climbed on his horse. The beauty of the valley filled his heart with joy.

John patted his chest, feeling the medicine bags of his father and Red Hawk. He smiled as he nudged his pony forward, and they began the slow descent toward his home. He thought about when Rusty had built that cabin of his with great care and fanfare, only to discover he couldn't sleep in it. He soon took to sleeping on the ground behind the cabin on a blanket and would quickly fall asleep under the stars. Only in the bitterest cold of winter did he sleep inside by his fireplace, and then he would leave the cabin windows open. For two weeks now,

Rusty had been up in the mountains sleeping on a bed of pine needles inside a *wickiup*; there was no civilizing that old man.

Swift Moon made slow time through the snow, but John didn't push his pony any harder. The snow was deep, and they would arrive home in time for their evening meal. They soon emerged from the heavily-treed high hills into a meadow where his homestead was again visible. Behind his house were a small storage shack and a stable with a wooden corral circling around it. There were three ponies huddled together against the Canadian winter.

A large Dakota style tipi sat behind the corral, just in front of the forest that sprung up again at the base of the hills behind John's place. A wisp of smoke could be seen curling through the tipi's vent and up into the clear blue sky.

"It looks like Uncle is making his stew again, Swift Moon," he said, patting the pinto on his neck. "Let's go. His stew will taste mighty good when we add this deer meat to it."

They resumed their ride. The land flattened out, and they found the wagon trail that ran along the river. It was much warmer riding as the sun was higher, and the trees blocked off the wind from the trail. John pushed the buffalo robe hood off his head and shook his braids loose. It had been getting too warm inside the buffalo robe made long ago for him by Calf Woman.

Although the river was still flowing, ice had formed almost to its middle, and the sun reflected brightly off of it. John looked away from the river to the other side of the road where his cornfield lay covered with snow. He raised a corn crop only to meet government requirements for homesteading. Even though they maintained the image of being farmers, Rusty and John really lived very much like in the old days. Their hunting and trapping skills kept them fed, and they sold their furs for any money they needed. John could have planted a much larger corn crop, but he chose to leave the land as he had found it when he, Wakala, and Rusty had fled from the Standing Rock reservation. Most of the valley was left in grass, where John grazed his small pony herd, and, secretly, hoped the buffalo would return.

As he approached the log cabin, he saw Wakala's face at the small window, smiling approvingly at him and the deer he carried. He waved at her. Wakala opened the curtain wider and held up a little black-haired girl, who waved excitedly at her father.

"Hello, Song of the Winds," he called to her as he passed the window and headed toward the shack to hang the deer for cleaning. The child continued waving until John vanished around the corner of the house. There, his two dogs ran up to greet him, barking and jumping. He hung the buck inside the wooden shack and chased the dogs outside while he slammed the doors shut.

"Where have you been, mongrels?" he laughed, the dogs jumping up on him. "Back with my uncle trying to beg a meal huh? Well, we will feed you soon enough. Now, get down."

John led Swift Moon into the stable where he slipped off his bridle and blanket and left the horse eating heartily from the hay. Trudging through the snow, he opened the door and entered his cabin.

The inside was not arranged like a white man's home. The corners were covered with buffalo hide so that it was not square, but a large circle, much like the inside of a tipi. The log walls were painted with buffalo, deer, and Dakota legends, all drawn by Wakala. The beds, made from pine needles and covered with blankets, were on the dirt floor. They were spread around the walls, centered on the black, pot-bellied stove.

Song of the Winds ran up to John, and she jumped into his arms. He grabbed the two-year-old girl and hugged her to his chest, swinging her around.

"*Ho*, my Little Singing Bird, have you missed your father while I hunted for deer?" he asked.

She only giggled and nodded her head. Squirming, she slipped from his hands and ran across the room to Wakala. John ran after her and grabbed Wakala in a hug.

"How have you been while I was gone, Wakala?" he asked his wife.

"I have been fine, but I am always lonesome when you are gone." He squeezed her hand; their affection for each other had grown stronger over the years.

"I have missed you too," he told her. "Now, where is that son of mine? I have been hunting three days, and he is not here to see his father returning from a successful hunt.

"Little Frog!" he hollered. "Where are you hiding?"

"He can not hear you, Waukesha," Wakala told him. "He is out in the tipi with Iron Hatchet, and the old man is chanting again. All day he sings to Wakantanka to destroy the whites and bring back the buffalo, while Little Frog sits and listens to him."

"Ah, that is a fine song he sings," said John with a grin. "Too bad it cannot come true, as the white man is here to stay. We can only try to hold onto our past values and sacred beliefs and try to remain Dakotas at heart."

"I'm afraid many of our people on the reservations have forgotten the old ways," she said. "That is why they made a new chief to take Iron Hatchet's place."

"Yes, you are right," he said, seriously. "It is too bad I cannot return there to help my people."

"You are doing your best here, Waukesha. We live very much like in the old days, and you write down the tales that Iron Hatchet tells you. Someday your words will help our people understand the glory that was their ancestors."

He said nothing for a moment; deep inside, he knew he could never return to the Dakotas. He would be arrested. Only the use of his white name in Canada, and Sergeant Burton's influence, kept the authorities from finding him. He was a white man to the outside world.

"I will go and see the boy and Iron Hatchet," he told her as he opened the door. "Throw some venison in the stew, for I have this feeling Rusty will be back tonight. He has been gone for a couple of weeks and will be missing your coffee."

He closed the door behind him and walked across the snow toward Iron Hatchet's tipi, which sat back from the house, surrounded by trees. The tipi was very cold in the winter, but Iron Hatchet always slept there instead of in the cabin. He hated wood buildings because both of Iron Hatchet's wives had died of cholera while he lived in a cabin on Standing Rock Reservation. Iron Hatchet believed the stale air trapped inside the wooden cabin had killed them.

John thought of Chipeto and Calf Woman as he neared the tipi. They had both been very kind to him, treated him like he was their son, and now they were dead. They had died two years ago when a cholera epidemic swept parts of the reservation. Iron Hatchet had lost both of his wives, but he had continued fighting for his people until the agent bribed several young men to declare another brave as chief. The agent refused to deal with Iron Hatchet from that day on, and his power quickly faded. Either the people were forced to deal with the new chief or they were denied their rations. Soon, Iron Hatchet was left alone, with only his old friend Manter sticking by him.

Manter had told the Quaker, Mr. Taylor, that Iron Hatchet had relatives up in Canada and suggested that Iron Hatchet might be happier up there. A letter soon found its way to Sergeant Burton, and the necessary arrangements were made. Manter escorted his old friend off the reservation at night; some friends of the Quakers took him to Sergeant Burton at the border and into Canada to John's farm.

Waukesha entered the lodge of Iron Hatchet and saw the old man sitting by his fire, pounding on a small leather hand drum. He wore only a breechcloth as he sat chanting on his blanket. He was almost blind now, and he had lost most of his teeth.

Little Frog sat across from Iron Hatchet, listening to his great uncle's chant. He jumped up when his father entered.

"Father," he cried and ran into Waukesha's arms. "Did you bring home a grizzly bear for our supper?"

John smiled at his son. "No, no grizzly this time, but I did manage to kill a large deer for us."

"Oh, that's good!" the boy exclaimed. "Grizzly is too tough to eat anyway. Can I have the antlers?"

"I think so, Little Frog, unless your mother needs them for tools."

John took the boy's hand and led him over to Iron Hatchet, where they sat down next to him and crossed their legs. The old man reached out and touched John's face.

"Ahh, my son has returned with food for his family. You carry on as if the white man had never crossed our lands. Whenever I feel that the red man will be totally destroyed by the whites, I think of you, and I am not so sad."

"I do not think our people will be destroyed, Iron Hatchet," John reassured him. "Wakantanka will smile on us again someday, and we will again be free men."

"Those are fine words, Waukesha. I only hope they are true. You have killed a deer. May I have some meat for my stew?"

"Wakala is dressing the animal now. She shall bring you a fine cut soon."

The old man smiled broadly, the gaps in his teeth dark holes. "You are a fine son. It is too bad Little Horse is not here with us to enjoy this meal. He was as fine a brave that ever rode the Dakota prairie."

"Yes, he was, and he is still with us in spirit. When Little Frog becomes a man, we will change his name to Little Horse.

"Uncle, Rusty is coming back tonight, and we want you to join us for the meal. Afterwards, we will talk over the old days. I need to write everything down for our people, so they will always know they are Dakotas."

"I will be there," the old man answered. "Rusty knows as many of the old stories as I do, and he makes my heart glad when he tells them. Are you sure he is all white?" Iron Hatchet asked.

"He is *wasicun* on the outside, but his heart is pure Dakota," John answered. "Come, Little Frog, let's return to our lodge. If we work fast enough, we may have your bow finished before supper is ready."

They started eating supper shortly after the sun went down. Sitting on the ground, they ate out of clay plates. It was quiet in the cabin. They were all a little disappointed that Rusty hadn't shown up. Darkness settled in, and he probably wouldn't be traveling this late.

The temperature dropped outside while a light snow fell, but, as a fire roared in the stone fireplace and the iron stove radiated its own heat, the cabin felt warm. The children finished eating and joyfully crawled on John as he tried to eat a piece of venison. Little Frog climbed on his father's shoulders, and John flipped him onto the blanket, the two of them laughing.

Suddenly, John heard something. "Be still, little ones," he whispered. He stood up and walked to the door and listened.

"It's Rusty!" he proclaimed, and they all ran to the door and stepped outside. A voice could be heard coming from the darkness across the river.

"Hey, Waukesha, I'm coming in. Save me some supper and get the coffee brewing." The booming voice carried clearly through the snow and wind.

Soon, a large figure could be seen through the snow as Rusty walked over the mostly frozen creek and up the bank. Two dozen furs were slung over his shoulders; he looked like a huge bear wearing snowshoes as he halted in front of them. He laid the furs down, grinning proudly at the fox furs, weasel and beaver pelts, and several minks.

"Look at this fine bunch of hides I got us this time, Little Frog!" Rusty shouted as he picked up the half-naked boy. "Why, hell, there's enough money here to buy us all the fastest ponies in Canada."

"You have done well again," John said, pounding his friend on his back. "There aren't many trappers as good as you."

He bent down and picked up the furs. "C'mon in, Rusty. We just started eating the deer I killed this morning, and I think there's enough for you."

"Sounds good," Rusty said, picking up Song of the Winds in his other arm. "And how you been, little princess?" he asked the girl with a squeeze. She laughed in response.

They entered the warm cabin where Iron Hatchet still sat chewing his supper.

"Hey, White Hair," he called out to Rusty. "Where you been so long a time? Don't tell me a little snow like this slowed the great hunter down."

Rusty brushed the snow off his coat and hat as he took them off. He had kicked off his snowshoes outside. He was sixty summers old, but still strong and robust. His hair was as white as ever, his wrinkles somewhat deeper, but his eyes still sparkled blue.

"I guess maybe I'm gettin' a little older, Chief," he answered Iron Hatchet, "and it takes my tired legs longer to climb those hills out there."

Rusty sat down next to his old friend, and, reaching inside his deerskin shirt, pulled out two cigars. Lighting them one after the other, he handed the first to Iron Hatchet. The old chief puffed deeply and blew the smoke out slowly, obviously enjoying himself.

"Fine cigar," Iron Hatchet said. "Only good white man invention besides coffee."

"Glad you like it," Rusty said, as he took a draw off his cigar. The others had taken their places in the circle and sat listening to the two old men.

"How you been feeling, Chief?"

The chief took another puff before answering. "Oh, pretty good for so old a man as I am. Sometimes I am very lonely for the old days and my old friends."

"Yeah, I know what you mean."

"Sometimes," Iron Hatchet continued, "I can almost believe that my dead brothers are with me. I have even found myself talking to Calf Woman before I realize she is dead." He was quiet for a minute.

"It is very lonesome."

The room was silent now. All but the children had fond memories of Calf Woman and Chipeto, and it saddened them, especially because their bones were so far away from them.

Finally, John spoke softly. "Wakala, bring Rusty some coffee. He's had a long cold journey."

"Yeah, Wakala, I sure have missed that coffee of yours. When I make it, it tastes like buffalo glue."

Wakala stood up and went to the stove. She poured a tin cup full of coffee and handed it to Rusty.

"Here," she said. "Warm yourself as your presence warms our house."

"Thank you," the big man answered, taking the steaming hot cup.

"It is good to have you back again, Rusty," John told him. "These are good times when we are all together. It does not seem like such bad times for my people when we meet and talk over the past." The mood slowly lightened as Rusty and Iron Hatchet drank coffee and smoked their cigars.

John got his paper to make notes. When Iron Hatchet and Rusty talked, the adventures and legends of the past came to life vividly, and he tried to write it all down. It would be his contribution to his people's culture.

Little Frog sat down next to his great uncle, putting his hand on his knee. "Uncle Iron Hatchet, tell us a new story tonight, please. Tell us about fighting the Crows in the old days."

"Ahh, my son," Iron Hatchet answered him, "let me see. Oh, I know a good story, full of brave deeds and heroics. I think maybe even Rusty doesn't know this story."

The old man looked at John and smiled. "Several summers back," Iron Hatchet continued, "a young man came to live with the Hunkpapa Dakota for a summer. He was a Dakota, but had been raised by the whites, and he wanted to know more about his people. So, we took him in, taught him to track the deer, hunt the buffalo, and live like a free man should live.

"One morning while he was in our camp, the Crows raided our pony herd and stole several fine ponies, including the war pony of Manter.

"This young man was selected to go with the Hunkpapa to raid the Crows, and win back our ponies and our glory."

John smiled and laid the note pad down on the floor. He knew this tale was his adventures in the Crow raid of his first Dakota summer, and he wouldn't need to take notes. He reached over and squeezed Wakala's hand as Song of the Winds came and sat on his lap.

No, life isn't so bad, he thought. He turned his attention back to Iron Hatchet as the chief continued on with his tale. John closed his eyes and he could hear the horses thundering across the Dakota plains. He could see Little Horse riding next to him, Manter leading the way. Ah, the glory of it all!

The End

ABOUT THE AUTHOR

Richard L. DuMont is a lifelong resident of Cincinnati, Ohio. He is a graduate of Xavier University, and a Vietnam veteran. Married, he has children and grandchildren.

His passion for Native Americans and their culture began as a young man and eventually led to writing this novel.

CPSIA information can be obtained
at www.ICGtesting.com
Printed in the USA
FFHW022152140319
51024571-56429FF